DON'T STAND OUT!!!

By

Waleed Simba

DON'T !

STAND !!

**FORMER
US MARINE
SERGEANT**

**FORMER
UNDERCOVER
NARCOTICS
OFFICER**

OUT !!!

BLACK BELT !

BY WALEED SIMBA

ISBN: 1-4107-8741-9 (e-book)
ISBN: 1-4107-8740-0 (Paperback)
ISBN: 1-4140-3347-8 (Dust Jacket)

This book is printed on acid free paper.

1stBooks – rev. 11/17/03

Dedication

This book is dedicated to Mrs. Annie Lois White Thompson Davis, mother/matriarch (deceased).

"Don't Stand Out" was chosen as the title of this book for three main reasons.

The first reason is that when I was a child, my mother encouraged me to be the best that I could be at whatever I did and, at the same time, not to be a braggart or bring attention to myself.

The second reason is that I have learned since I began to study martial arts some thirty years ago that there is not enough time to totally master a martial art, so it must be a lifetime study. As a student of the martial arts, you realize that there will always be someone better and that the goal is not to be better than the next guy, but rather to improve yourself in every way. Hopefully, as you progress, you find ways to improve others' lives just by exposing them to you as a true martial artist.

The third and final reason is that as an undercover police officer the whole idea was to blend in and not be different from the people on the street. This is a most important component of the trade as it can be fatal if you do, "stand out."

A big reason to move to Cabo Master
Caught This 10 ½ foot – 155lbs marlin June/1996

Written by student and friend Vickey Lindemann

Forward

by

Vickey Lindemann

Taekwondo was first introduced to me in Cabo San Lucas, B.C.S., Mexico as a class offered to children at one of our local spas, to which I was a member. It looked like something I wanted to get my two daughters to get involved with. I had heard of karate and judo and different martial arts, but did not know the difference. The class was held in an aerobics room, which could accommodate about ten kids. I introduced myself to the instructor, Waleed Simba, and told him I was interested in signing my girls up. He said he had only a few uniforms and space left in the class and my girls; ages 12 and 14 were excited to be involved. The class quickly filled. Raising children in a foreign country, you do not always find a very good selection of activities available, and the interest level for this type of activity in the small tourist town of Cabo San Lucas was high. I would watch the children do their exercises and kicks saw how much they all enjoyed taking the classes. Master Simba was really good with the children and was emphasizing the discipline that goes along with this art. He explained the importance of knowing the history of Taekwondo and the phrases used in this art.

Master Simba soon saw the need to relocate to a larger location, and opened his kwan (school) and offered classes to all ages; offering three classes a week for each group. I have always been an active person, and enjoyed several different types of physical activities. I saw this as an opportunity to learn a martial art with my children, not realizing that what I would learn was how to discipline myself in mind and body. I was 38 years old when I began the class, and found myself going more than three times per week. I found it very challenging to push my body through the exercises, and then the kicks, which grew more difficult each month. But my body was growing stronger and more fit than I had ever been before, and this made me feel good about myself. We were always preparing for our next belt tests, and this was challenging to all the students. At times, it was frustrating, but Master Simba was able to push us and teach us in a way to keep us going. It definitely wasn't all fun and games. I am not sure what belt level I was practicing for when it was announced Master Kim, would come and grade our next test. This was very exciting and made our Taekwondo experience even more of a reality. Master Kim was one of Simba's teachers in Seattle. I found I really enjoyed learning the different forms, and though I learned all the movements, I found I wasn't as coordinated with the smooth graceful art of Taekwondo and that it would take many many years of practice to find that grace.

One of the areas of Taekwondo that had me nervous at my age was sparring. That is the actual combat of two people. We had all the correct protective gear necessary and I participated and practiced, but I did not enjoy this area as much as the younger male students. However, the self-defense techniques involved in fighting will be helpful to me throughout the rest of my life. I put a lot of concentration into learning all the new kicks, punches and forms necessary to pass each belt level and my confidence in my physical self grew. Another part of working towards your black belt was to teach. I did not feel confident in doing this at first, as I felt I still had so much to learn and practice myself. However, with the schools continued growth to approximately 60 plus students, Master Simba assigned classes for the advanced students to teach. First we began by leading our own classes, and then my oldest daughter and I began teaching other classes. After working hard and learning the different kicks, punches, forms and self defense techniques, I was able to graduate through the different belt levels. Master Simba announced that Master Han would come to Cabo San Lucas to observe and grade those students testing for their black belts. As there were six of Master Simba's first students prepared to test, this was exciting, as well as a great privilege and honor for each of us. I couldn't believe I could achieve my first-degree black belt in a year, but know I put a lot time and hard energy into practicing and passing each level. During our black belt test, each student testing must read a handwritten page they wrote about what Taekwondo meant to them. I remember writing my paper and feeling nervous to read it in front of all the friends and families who attended the testing that day. You are required to turn your paper in as part of the test, to the World Taekwondo Federation and I wish I had made a copy for myself. I do not remember what I wrote now, but now that I felt really good about it. There were five of us to receive our black belt certifications and it was really exciting to receive and tie on our black belts in front of friends and family, each belt having our names embossed on them. This was quite an accomplishment for me having suffered a serious injury six years earlier. My oldest daughter and I achieved this unbelievable goal together, while my other daughter practiced at her own pace.

Master Han seemed quite a bit younger than Master Kim, both seeming to have quiet characteristics, but emanating a great presence. Master Han stayed after our black belt test for a couple days and taught some of his techniques to the students. This was an unexpected treat for everyone. I continued taking and teaching classes and working towards my second-degree black belt during the next year. I also helped Master Simba with the new students while they took their different level tests. Teaching seemed to be more and more of my training, and I was filling in on a fairly regular basis or when Master Simba was gone. It seemed like I was teaching more than I was receiving help with my training and this took some of my enjoyment of the art away. I continued to teach classes several times a week and was soon to test for my second-degree black belt. My next test was going to be another big event, as Master Simba was trying to arrange for some students from Korea to come to Cabo and put on a demonstration for all those interested. There were banners and t—shirts made, reservations for a convention room and ticket sales for admission. It looked like it was all going to come together and then at the last minute, the Korean students were unable to come. This was a big disappointment to everyone. I am sure even more so to Master Simba. Master Sirnba moved to La Paz. Master Simba found a great location in the center of town and opened his second school. The school in Cabo closed within two months. Although I would have liked to continue my training, and someday may, driving two hours one way was not feasible. I feel my girls and I have learned many valuable gifts from our involvement in Taekwondo and know it will always be a part of our lives, whether we are practicing or not.

Master Simba has moved on with his life and no longer is located in Mexico, but he is still a friend to our family and we continue to keep in contact with each other. VSLinCSL03/02

THAT MAN IS A SUCCESS

Author unknown

That man is a success, who has lived well, laughed often and loved much. Who has enjoyed the love of beautiful women, the respect of intelligent men and the admiration of children. Who has filled his niche and accomplished his tasks. Who leaves the world better than he found it, whether by an improved poppy, a perfect poem or a rescued soul. Who has never lacked appreciation of the Earth's' beauty or failed to express it. Who has always looked for the best in others and gave the best that he had; who life was an inspiration and whose memory a benediction.

Seattle Police Department

Norman H. Stamper, Chief of Police
Norman B. Rice, Mayor

July 16, 1996

RE: Detective Waleed Simba

To Whom It May Concern:

Waleed Simba was hired as a Seattle Police Officer on January 5, 1982. He brought excellent credentials from the United States Marine Corp.

Shortly after he completed his Academy training, he was assigned to work in an undercover capacity. He then served over seven years in the patrol division where he received numerous commendations. He, along with three other police officers, were the original members of our Seattle Police Street Narcotics Team. Waleed worked successfully with the Drug Enforcement Agency and other police agencies in dealing with drug related problems. Waleed also worked undercover with our Anti-Fencing Unit and on a Violent Burglaries Project. During this time, he worked with the Department of Agriculture and gained valuable experience in electronic and motor surveillance. Over the past five years, Waleed has worked as a Juvenile detective. In this capacity he worked with families of troubled youth to resolve problems between parents and children.

I offer my highest praise for Waleed's outstanding work with the Seattle Police Department and his commitment to the communities he served.

Sincerely,

Norm Stamper
Chief of Police

cc: personnel file

An equal employment opportunity - affirmative action employer
Reasonable accommodation for people with disabilities provided on request. Call (206) 684-5374 at least two weeks in advance.
City of Seattle Police Department 610 Third Avenue, Seattle, Washington 98104-1886
Printed on Recycled Paper

xiv

Seattle Police Department
Individual Training Record

Total Number of Reported Training Hours   881

Serial	Name	SSN:
4828		

Course	Name	Hrs	Course Date(s)	
293	Basic Law Enforcement Training	440	3/23/1982	3/23/1982
45	Emergency Vehicle Operation Course (EVOC)	24	3/29/1982	3/29/1982
155	Neck Restraint Training	8	5/6/1983	5/6/1983
67	Professional Skills Review	24	2/24/1984	2/24/1984
13	First Aid, Recertification	9	3/6/1985	3/6/1985
16	Driver Training - Refresher	16	4/1/1985	4/1/1985
53	Investment in Excellence	24	10/23/1985	10/23/1985
4	Breathalizer	4	2/25/1986	2/25/1986
2	BAC-Verifier, Basic	16	2/25/1986	2/25/1986
711	Gang Seminar	20	9/17/1988	9/17/1988
224	ACCESS/WACIC Level 1	8	12/4/1989	12/4/1989
13	Fhe, Aid, Recertification	8	1/3/1990	1/3/1990
90	Verbal Judo	8	6/13/1990	6/13/1990
90	Verbal Judo	8	6/20/1990	6/20/1990
90	Verbal Judo	8	6/21/1990	6/21/1990
90	Verbal Judo	8	6/22/1990	6/22/1990
178	Verbal Judo 4, Instructor	32	6/22/1990	6/22/1990
1315	Interview & Interrogation Techniques	24	12/18/1990	12/18/1990
15	AIDS, Hepatitis & Hazardous Materials	8	1/23/1991	1/23/1991
90	Verbal Judo	8	2/13/1991	2/13/1991
1315	Interview & Interrogation Techniques	24	2/20/1991	2/20/1991
14	Semi-Automatic Pistol Transitional Training	9	3/13/1991	3/16/1991
241	Instructor Development	40	12/13/1991	12/13/1991
30	Community Relations & Diversity Skills Training	16	4/22/1992	4/22/1992
411	Criminal Investigative Analysis	16	4/28/1992	4/28/1992
13	First Aid, Recertification	8	11/4/1992	11/4/1992
36	Exposure Control	2	3/2/1993	3/2/1993
1	Access/WACIC	2	6/29/1993	6/29/1993
79	Reid Method of Interviewing & Interrogation	24	12/15/1993	12/15/1993
36	Exposure Control	1	12/21/1993	12/21/1993
148	Glock Transition Training	16	1/13/1995	1/13/1995

XV

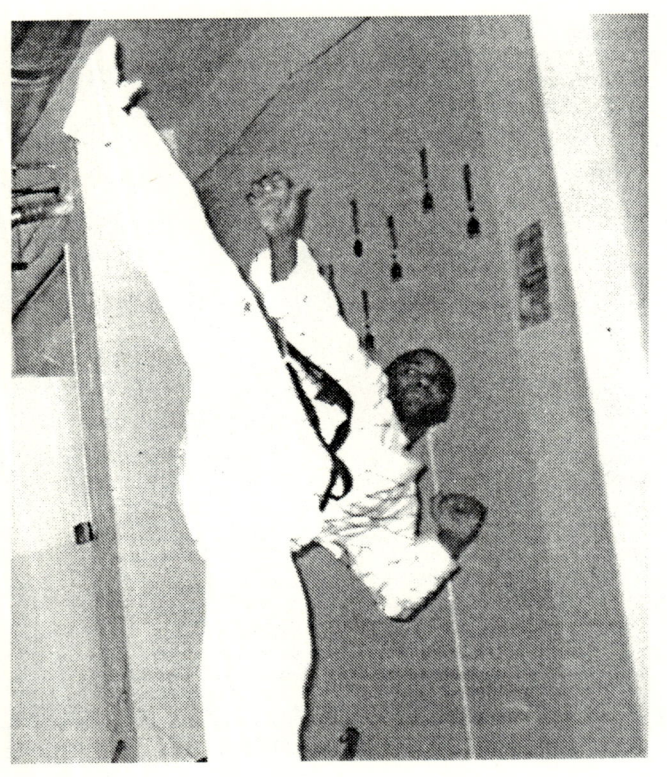

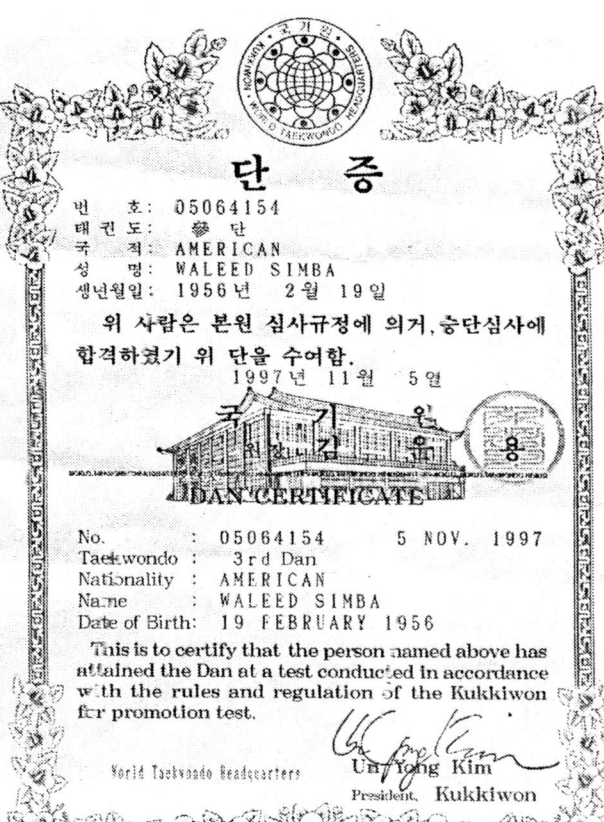

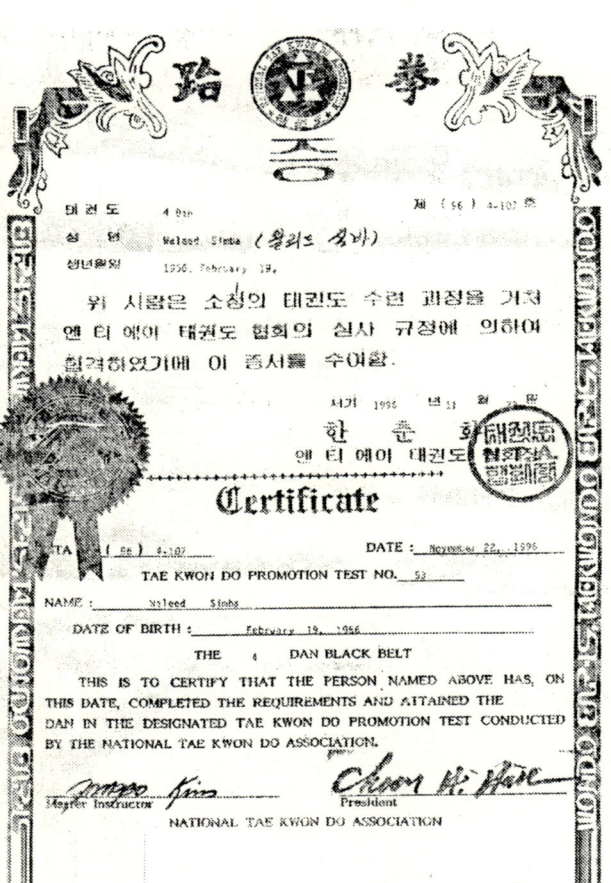

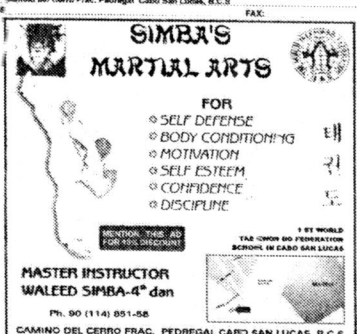

SIMBA'S TAEKWONDO
Camine Af *Cerre* S/N
Col. Pedregal. Cabo San Lucas, B.C.S.
C. P. 23410

TaeKwonDo

"Korean Tigers" Demonstration Team to visit Cabo San Lucas

In February 1999, SimBa's TaeKwonDo will sponsor the world famous "Korean Tigers Demonstration Team here in Cabo San Lucas and San Jose' Del Cabo. The "Tigers" travel the globe taking the thrills and excitement of true TaeKwonDo everywhere they go. This professional group of masters and black Belts perform various high flying kicking acrobatics as well as some of the best self defense demonstrations of the martial arts. There are also some of the best exhibitions of breaking techniques for speed and power.

SimBa's TaeKwonDo opened in Cabo San Lucas in 1996. operating under the rules of the World TaKwonDo Federation. Thus far. two Korean Masters have visited the school and several more are planned. The visit by the "Korean Tigers" is unprecedented as they are highly requested worldwide and without the assistance of Master Han and GrandMaster Yun of Seoul, Korea, this visit would not have been possible.

Until this event, SimBa's TaeKwonDo has stayed from competitions and demonstrations. This event will be the catalyst to more TaeKwondo activities in the Los Cabos area and introduce some of our students to World Class TaeKwonDo.

Organizations or individuals interested in future sponsorship of such events can contact Sabumnim Waleed SimBa or any of the Black Belts of SimBa's TaeKwondo.

Local TaeKwonDo Studio Hosting International Event

■ **With some very big names in the sport visiting us**

Local TaeKwonDo studio, headed by Waleed Simba, is sponsoring some famous practitioners of the art on a junket to Los Cabos.

Simba, who, despite the funny name, is a Gringo, explains that the Korean Tigers have agreed to come to Los Cabos specifically for a benefit for his school. TaeKwonDo is a kind of martial arts performed in the white jammie outfits held together by the belts of different colors denoting the level of achievement

The acrobatics and stunts you see in the martial arts movies are performed by these guys, and they are the best of the best. The team travels the world demonstrating TaeKwonDo, and this is a real honor to have them stop by here.

The visit was arranged with the help of Simba's master, Han Jai Hee and with the help of Mr. Hee's master, grandmaster Yun, both of Seoul, Korea.

The team consists of about 15 members and three dignitaries. Simba is seeking sponsors to help with the costs, as he must guarantee the gate.

The group will perform various high flying kicking acrobatics as well as some of the best self defense demonstrations of the martial arts. There are also some of the best exhibitions of breaking techniques for speed and power

Simba's TaeKwonDo studio opened in Cabo San Lucas in 1996, operating under the rules of the World TaeKwonDo Federation. The masters will be here Feb. 25 through March 1 and The events will be held Feb 27 and 28,

For more information, call Simba at 358 46 or cellular 85158. ❏

This song inspired and written by Waleed Simba in 1985 whileworking undercover in Narcotics:

ROCK HOUSE BLUES

WEEL—YOU KNOW IT STARTED ONE DAY
WHEN I WAS FEELIN KINDA BLUE
PUSHERMAN CAME AROUND
HE SAID, "I GOT SOMETHIN FOR YOU"

TOOK A LOOK AT MYSELF
ASKED WHAT I HAD TO LOSE
AND THAT'S WHEN IT STARTED
"THE ROCK HOUSE BLUES"

I GOT THE ROCK HOUSE BLUES
IT HAPPENS WHEN YOU USE
TALKIN BOUT ROCK HOUSE BLUES
YOU CAN'T WIN, YOU ONLY LOSE

BEFORE I REALLY KNEW IT
I WAS HOOKED ON THAT PIPE
I WOULD FOLLOW THAT BOWL
FROM DAY INTO NIGHT

WHEN MY LAST DAY CAME
I WAS HIGHER THAN BEFORE
I COULDN'T MOVE
THERE WAS A KNOCK AT THE DOOR

THE DOOR FELL DOWN
POLICE CAME CRASHING IN
AS FAR AS I KNOW
THAT DAY DIDN'T END
IN AN UNCONSCIENOUS STATE
I HEARD SOME HEARTSTOPPING NEWS
THEY SAID THAT THAT GUY DIED
OF THE ROCK HOUSE BLUES

HE HAD THE ROCK HOUSE BLUES
HE WAS DEAD, TOES UP
IT HAPPENS WHEN YOU USE
ROCK HOUSE BLUES
GONE TO ROCK HEAVEN
ROCK HOUSE BLUES
ROCK GOT HIM, HE'S HISTORY
ROCK HOUSE BLUES
ROCK HOUSE BLUES
ROCK HOUSE BLUES

Introduction

It was my fortieth birthday, a time to reflect. I had been a police officer and detective for over fourteen years. In the last year, a friend and fellow officer had been killed, and most recently, my mother had passed away.

From the time I was a little boy, I prepared to be a good American. I joined the Cub Scouts and later the Boy Scouts. I then followed my four older brothers into the United States Marine Corps where I spent over six years. I was a sergeant when I received my medical discharge. After over a year working for the U.S. Customs Service in an entry level position as well as doing some very hard work to recover from my military career-ending injury, I recovered, became, and remained a police officer. I also hold a fourth degree black belt in TaeKwonDo.

The above mentioned friend and I studied martial arts at the same school. At times I would give him personal advice about the arts and he also liked to hear about some of my exploits as an undercover narcotics officer. He had had about three years on the department and had recently been transferred to the narcotics section as an undercover agent. He took pride in his abilities as a cop and his physical abilities as well.

I used to think that he absorbed TaeKwonDo a little too easily and discovered later that he had been a contemporary dancer. He used to tell me that he would achieve his black belt in less time than it took most. I believed him because of his commitment and dedication to practice. When something was difficult for him, he just worked that much harder.

We worked on the same floor in the East Precinct of the Seattle Police Department. He used to come to my desk over in the juvenile section after lunch almost daily and quiz me. I liked his enthusiasm and his questions kept me on my toes.

On the other hand, my mother was my connection to the "Great Spirit." She was a very religious woman and incredibly spiritual. From her, I learned that there is a big difference between the two. She had raised me to be a good boy and ensured that I went to church every Sunday while growing up. I was even a Sunday school teacher. She watched as I grew spiritually and she seemed to know that I was seeking my own way in this life. She was there for me and I know I broadened her senses with some of my discoveries.

My mother didn't talk much about herself. I discovered that she had had a hard life, but a satisfying one. My mother was part white, part Cherokee, and part black. My great-grandmother was white. My grandfather was Cherokee Indian. My mother and all of her siblings looked like proud tall Native Americans and I always wanted to know more about the Cherokee side of the family.

I remember when I transitioned into Al-Islam my mother was so worried that I was going to become an enemy of the white man and that I was going to follow the honorable minister Louis Farrakhan to the ends of the Earth. As she lived in North Carolina and I lived in Seattle, we would speak on the phone regularly — not regularly enough for her, I might add. So during one of these conversations about life, she made one of her comments about the minister. I decided to carefully address her knowledge of him.

I asked what she knew about him other than what the media had told her. After she got over her defensiveness, she understood that I was not challenging her, but asking her to open up her mind. I asked her to listen to the minister's weekly broadcast that week and we could talk about it afterward.

Well, she phoned me after she had listened to him and she was so proud. She was proud of me for looking outside what had been pushed at me all those years and discovering that I was on the road to finding myself. She was proud of the minister for being so eloquent, educated, articulate, commanding, beautiful and black. She had only known black leaders to be like the Reverend Dr. Martin Luther King. Don't misunderstand, we both loved him, but a black man who would confront society with no fear, just "truth," was something new.

That was what was wonderful about my mother. She was strong and had no use for big mouths with empty heads. But when she had cause to consider something, she gave credit where it was due.

She and I had fishing in common and would regularly talk a lot about the fishing that we were both doing.

In June 1996, I was in Cabo San Lucas, Mexico. I was still feeling the losses of both my mother and my friend. I was on a spiritual search. I was with my girlfriend, but I was also very alone. I had the opportunity to catch a great striped marlin (fish). It weighed one hundred fifty-five pounds and was ten feet, six inches long. It was a great catch and I took what I would eat home to the U.S. and shared the rest with the local people.

While I was reeling that fish in, which took an hour, I had a real conversation with my mother. At the time she had been deceased for about three months, but I knew that she was there watching me. One of the questions that I asked her was if she had caused that fish to bite my line and had given me that opportunity. I knew she was there and she was happy for me.

After the fish was boated and the excitement was coming to a close, I realized that I had had a conversation with a person that was not physically present. I discreetly explored everyone's expression to see if I was being evaluated as some kind of nut. I could not tell and it did not matter anyway. I also knew that when that captain asked me if I wanted to mount the fish as a trophy that it was not God's intention for that magnificent creature to sacrifice his life to be put on a wall. In total truth, I appreciated that great being every time I had a meal of him.

Chapter One

I was lucky number eleven, born February 19, 1956. My life had an interesting start. You see the ten siblings before me seemed to be well adjusted, although I couldn't figure out the tenth one. It seemed he hated me from day one.

I had friends who had big brothers and those big brothers would never let anyone mess with their little brothers. Not so in my case, other people didn't get an opportunity to mess with me because my brother had the market on kicking my butt. He would beat me up anywhere and in front of anyone, except family. This wasn't just an isolated thing; it was all the time.

He was really clever; he would never do anything to me in the presence of other family members. I am glad I don't remember my infancy, as I am sure it must have started there.

As I got a little older, I started to recognize the abuse for what it was. There were several early warning signs. Growing up in a one-parent home with as many kids as we had in our home, there was no time for slackers. Everyone had chores. The little ones like me, my next older brother and one sister were close in age and too young to work real jobs. We had to wash dishes, sweep and mop floors, take out garbage, rake leaves, and clean our rooms. I constantly found myself doing my chores and my brother's. He would always seem to have something to threaten to tell on me or would just plain make me do his share of the chores. He used to hurt me a lot and for no reason most of the time. He just seemed to enjoy it.

I remember trying to get him to like me. Sometimes I would hang around his friends, who were also my friends when he wasn't around, and they liked me fine. Then he would come around and chase me home. I would usually be crying. Our friends couldn't understand it either. He had to have all the attention. It was explained to me this way. He had been the baby before I came along and he resented me for it — forever.

I remember thinking all the time when I was in my teen years that if my life was being made this hard by a family member, then it must be really tough when I grew up and got out on my own. I even had a girlfriend in junior high that

I really liked. One day she just stopped talking to me and treated me like some kid. Shortly after that, I discovered she was going out with my brother.

Well, time went on and I continued to grow up. I was always adventurous, but afraid of everything. In junior high school I went out for the football team with my friends and I made the team. My brother ridiculed and degraded me until I quit. Granted, I was an average player with a few skills, but my friends were no better than I was or maybe not as good. When we played sandlot, I was pretty good and I was sure it could carry over to organized football. I just didn't have the confidence to pursue anything that would put me in a position of attention.

After my short-lived football career, I began TaeKwonDo classes at a nearby martial arts school. Three of my friends started at the same time. Two of them were on the same football team mentioned above. They were not the better players and in fact did not stand out at all. We all really liked TaeKwonDo and were pretty competitive.

I failed my first belt promotion for my yellow belt. My friends, the other would-be football players —excuse me, those not so good football players — passed that test. My master told me that it was my attitude not my ability. I continued to practice and found myself to be quite in agreement with Tae Kwon Do.

When I got to high school, I tried out for the football team again. Then I quit again. I thought, *Damn, I can't keep quitting things.*

I had four older brothers who were all U.S. Marines. I decided I would join and learn to finish what I started for once. So I joined to the chagrin of all who knew me.

I played a dirty little trick on my mother. You see, I had a high school girlfriend and we were pretty close. Our families were close as well. They all wanted us to marry right out of school. I knew that wasn't for me. I did not tell anyone that I was going into the Marines and I secretly planned my getaway.

Upon speaking with one of my older brothers, who was also a Marine working in the testing office for new enlistees, I knew that I did not want to be in the infantry. I knew the questions to ask and, upon completing the testing, it was discovered that I had an aptitude for the mechanical and electrical occupational specialty. In short we called this a motor transport mechanic (MOS 3521).

School was out the end of June and I had the option to leave for Parris Island on the first of July 1974 or the seventh of July. I decided that I wanted to spend the fourth of July with my family and friends even though I still hadn't told anyone my plans.

On the night of July sixth, I told my mother that I had gotten a new job. I asked her to wake me early in the morning. I then went into the bathroom and shaved my head. My mother awakened me as I had requested. She made me breakfast. When I came out to eat, I was wearing some old khakis, a white T-shirt and an old pair of Converse tennis shoes.

My mother asked, "Where are you going to work looking like that?"

I laughed and avoided answering her question. Shortly after that, there was a knock at the front door. My mother answered the door to a Marine Corps gunnery sergeant. Realizing that my new job was the United States Marine Corps, my mother began to cry. I felt really bad because what I thought had been a joke had made her feel bad. She regrouped and

4

acknowledged that she knew that I would probably go into the Marines one day, just not that soon.

We had a special moment and cried together and I left to become a man.

My mother was always my best friend. She believed in me and encouraged me in everything. She was afraid for me and was very protective. Even though she knew that I would probably leave one day, she had hoped that I would marry my girlfriend and remain at home. She also told me throughout her life that I could do whatever I set my mind to. My mother instilled in me a spirit that was stronger than the negativity that surrounded blacks in the South.

My mother had had a hard upbringing herself. You see, she was the eleventh child of twelve children.

My grandfather, her father, was Cherokee Indian. My grandmother, her mother, was half-white. My great-grandmother was white, and as such, especially during this era, they were not readily accepted in either culture.

We grew up in black neighborhoods and there was always a feeling of not quite belonging. I didn't realize at the time that we were not like regular black people. I would discover much about this later. I left home to discover the world and to fulfill my destiny. I had that Great Spirit inside that allowed me to handle my fears and step out into the world.

As any Marine knows, the Marine Corps Recruit Depot in Parris Island, South Carolina is where traditional U.S. Marines are born. The other ones we call "Hollywood Marines." Of course, I was born on Parris Island.

Upon my arrival for my initial three months basic training, I was immediately assigned to a platoon of approximately ninety recruits. We were rapidly herded through processing and issued our work uniforms, boots, and essentials. I was number 82, which put me at the end of the line most of the time. So by the time I got issued anything, it was too small or too large or they were just plain out. When I received my sneakers, they were out of size tens and they gave me a size eight and told me to be quiet and keep the line moving.

It was lunch time and time for our first meal on Parris Island. We were herded over to the chow hall. There were recruits all around us that had been there for various periods of time and they looked good as they marched and did everything as a group. We were told that we weren't even good enough to look at them. The drill instructors called us the "Mob."

There was also a big difference when the seasoned platoons marched in. They were proud and marched lean and mean. When they came to a stop in front of us, they sounded like one big giant explosion as their heels came together at the last step. Pop!

When we had been herded over to chow, we looked like misfits. The command for us to stop was not very commanding and the drill instructors surrounded us. They screamed and totally humiliated us in front of God and everybody. Everyone in our platoon was so destroyed.

To top everything off, as we came to a stop in front of the chow hall, our sensitive drill instructor shouted out those soon to be familiar words. "Hippity hop, mob stop."

As I told you before, I had three brothers in the Corps when I went in. One of them was a drill instructor — that's right, on Parris Island. Well, I saw him as we mobbed into the chow hall. Now, mind you, he was not my nemesis, but one of my other brothers that had been good to me. We were told only to look in front and not to "eyeball," which meant to look around. Well, I did look around and who did I find looking me in the eye? I gave a slight smile; expecting one in return. He not only smiled, he laughed out loud. He then proceeded to run in my direction. I noticed that he was not coming alone, but with about four or five other drill instructors. Yes, my brother was a drill instructor first.

I realized the closer he got that he was not happy to see me. He began to yell like a crazy man as did the others and I really didn't understand it. I surmised it was because I was "eyeballing." They wouldn't let me apologize. They cut into me until I was totally disoriented. Then my brother happened to look down at my feet and noticed that my sneakers were untied and too small. It started all over again. I just wanted to be anywhere else.

They finally let me go inside and eat. Luckily, my brother was not one of my drill instructors, he was in third battalion and I was in first. I didn't know exactly what that meant. I just knew he wouldn't be around all the time. After our first meal, we were herded back to our barracks. There we were given free time to write home, take showers, shine boots and make our bunks. We had had a day of chaos and were ready to go to bed with clean sheets and clean, fresh underwear. Fresh!

The lights went out at ten p.m. and we were allowed to go to sleep. My luck wasn't to last. In the dark, a voice came from the quarterdeck, which was the area from which drill instructors appeared. Now any Marine can tell you that drill instructors are indeed, "godlike." They appear out of thin air.

A voice called out my name. As was the requirement when a recruits' name was called, every other private had to repeat the name all together and instruct that particular recruit to report to the drill instructor. They did and I did. Upon reaching the quarterdeck, I was surprised to find my brother, the drill instructor. He calmly and quietly instructed me do a series of exercises until I was soaked in my own perspiration.

He laughed and told me, "Go climb in your fresh bed now."

My first night on Parris Island was like that. That first letter that I was allowed to write was to my mother.

I told her how my brother had treated me. I told her he was no longer my brother. I would finish in spite of him.

I won't even go into boot camp stories, suffice it to say, that is a whole other book. I graduated from boot camp and went on to my motor transport school to learn my new job. That course was given at Camp Johnson, which was an annex of Camp Lejeune, North Carolina (home of the Second Marine Division.) That was also a three-month course. The redeeming part of this course was that the same brother that had been at Parris Island had been reassigned to Camp Lejeune. So I had a pretty normal military life as his family was there with him. I had great meals every day and enjoyed time with his wife and boys.

I spent weekends there when I didn't drive home to my mother's house in Charlotte. I forgave him for being so hard on me on Parris Island; he just wanted me to be a good Marine.

Upon completion of that course, I was given orders to Okinawa. I grew up a bit more while I was overseas. I was shipped out on February 18, 1975. That was the day before my nineteenth birthday. We flew straight through my birthday. I hope that means I am a year younger, not!

I arrived there a private and was promoted shortly afterward to private first class. I was assigned to the Third Motor Transport Battalion at Camp Schwab. It was the northernmost base on the island. As a young Marine there, and my first real time away from home, I really enjoyed Okinawa. I took some martial arts classes at an Okinawan Kenpo school. I also had a group of Marines on the base who wanted me to give classes in TaeKwonDo. I was hardly an instructor, but we had good classes and I even realized I knew more than I thought. One of my students was a bit overbearing. He was a class clown. Even though likable, he embellished everything. He actually got the opportunity to put some of this training to use.

As a unit we went to Subic Bay, Philippines for liberty. At that time there was martial law in the

Philippines, which meant we could not be on the street after midnight. Our last night there, this particular Marine wanted to go to a party that would put us jeopardy of not getting back to our ship on time. We were leaving the next morning. The group decided against going to the party, but this guy went by himself.

Well, the next morning he was not there when we left the Philippines. We arrived back in Okinawa and heard that he had gotten into a fight at that party and had hurt a man very badly. The rumor was that the man had died from his injuries. Although this was never confirmed, we ceased practicing. That Marine returned to our unit about a week later.

Our company was gearing up to go on a "contingent," which was a peacekeeping deployment. An alternate duty was assisting in the recovery of the U.S. ship *Mayaquez*.

The Cambodian government had seized this ship. We would be supporting the Second Battalion Ninth Marine Regiment. There were twenty-some odd pieces of motor transport equipment. It ranged from five-ton wreckers down to one-quarter-ton jeeps. There were two squads of drivers and two mechanics.

One of the mechanics was a sergeant. He did drive the wrecker, but that was all he did. The other mechanic was a PFC (private first class). He did all the work on the vehicles for the entire deployment. He kept all those vehicles operational during embarkation and debarkation of U.S. naval vessels.

After returning from that deployment, the contingent was met by the regiment inspectors. Every one of those vehicles drove off under its own power. That was the first time that had happened since anyone could remember. The sergeant was congratulated and he happily accepted his accolades. He never acknowledged his young protégé.

However, on Monday after all the smoke had cleared, the motor transport chief informed the young lance corporal, who had been responsible for the work, that he had been told who was responsible for the vehicle readiness. That young lance corporal was meritoriously promoted to corporal. That twenty-year-old corporal was me.

After being stationed overseas for about ten months, I was contacted by the American Red Cross. My father had passed away and my mother requested that I come home.

When I got home, it was sad. Although I had not grown up with my father in my life, I had always wanted to know him. The only real memory that I had of my father was from a time when I was about four years old. It was a school day and all of my siblings were at school. A vending truck came by ringing his bell. I had developed a taste for Orange Crush. I was outside in the yard with my father as he was working on the front porch. I asked him to buy me an Orange Crush. He bought me a whole case and told me I could drink as much as I wanted but warned that I would get sick if I drank too much.

We buried my father and I asked questions that I had not been allowed to ask before. I got answers from my mother and my father's cousins and from some of my brothers and sisters. I was happy because I finally had an idea about who my father had been. I learned that I was a lot like him.

At the end of my visit home, I had seen my girlfriend once. Something was different between us, but I was not in a space to figure it out at that point. I returned to Okinawa to complete my tour of duty. When I got back to Okinawa, I had a letter from my girlfriend and she told me that she was pregnant. I knew that she had not gotten pregnant by me and I asked her for more information. She told me it was a guy that we had gone to school with. I was always glad that I was not in love with her because that would have destroyed me. She did, however, make my overseas assignment more bearable.

Prior to this development, she used to write me almost every day. She also used to send me cassettes and letters. She had been in a band with her brother and was a very good singer. I remember she recorded Minnie Rippertons' "Loving You" without any accompaniment. It was beautiful. She also became quite a celebrity with the guys in my platoon. They would gather around and I would read her letters out loud. They all called her name with familiarity and felt as though they knew her too. I never told her that, but I should have. She made all our lives easier for that year. When I say I was not in love with my girlfriend, it isn't to say I didn't care about what happened. She was probably more of a friend at that point and I was able to let her go.

I was lucky because I had been raised with six sisters.

They were artists in the way they controlled and manipulated the boyfriends and men in their lives. I watched as guys would come over one after the other and often times in the same day and night. Don't get me wrong, my sisters were each different. Although they were all beautiful and carried themselves as ladies, they were women. And part of being a woman was discovering your power over men. I learned a bit just by sitting back and observing.

I came back to the states a corporal. I then got a special assignment. I was sent to interview for the job as the commanding general's driver. I had never even seen a general before and wanted no part of a job like that. My sergeant major did not give me a choice. He told me to get a haircut and report to the general's office. I already had a regulation haircut and told him so. He told me the general liked clean heads with a little patch of hair on top. In the Marine Corps, we call this a "high and tight."

Well, I got my "high and tight" and reported to the general's office as directed. There were so many Marines there that I was relieved because I knew I did not stand a chance in hell of getting that job.

Finally I was called in. The general called me by my first name. He then proceeded to tell me we had served together overseas. I had never seen him before, but who was I to argue? He made me feel comfortable and the interview went well. He said he had others to interview, but he would let me know. I went back to my work area and resumed my duties.

I was the shop inspector, which meant I inspected the work of the mechanics. I worked for a very large, squared-away warrant officer. I think he liked me, but he would never admit it. Anyway, as that work day came to an end at 1600 hours, the warrant officer called me into his office.

He jokingly called me a "kiss ass" and congratulated me. I had already forgotten about the general and asked him what he was talking about. He told me that I was the general's new driver.

I was stunned. I knew nothing of the protocol of such an assignment. I knew that guys with these jobs were squared away Marines and I did not know if I measured up. None of my feelings mattered, I was selected and was to report the next working day. I was sent to cash sales to get issued some new dress blue uniforms.

On my first work day, I reported to the office to meet with his outgoing driver. This sergeant was super squared away. I thought, *Wow, I can never fill these shoes.*

He was nice and he was very patient as he trained me for a week. He showed me how to handle getting things done for the general. He taught me protocol. He taught me how to handle the types of events that would arise.

This job turned out to be the assignment of a lifetime. During my tenure as the general's driver, I worked for many VIPs and diplomats. I planned itineraries, made arrangements with transportation, and did whatever was necessary to make for smooth visits. Most of my activities were behind the scenes, but the general always thanked me because he knew I made his job easier. He entrusted me with many personal tasks as well and this made me proud that he trusted me. He even always sincerely asked about my mother.

I had many memorable moments with the general. My two most memorable moments were when on my twenty-first birthday, he called me into his office at the end of the day and quizzed me about my birthday activities. I was just elated that he even knew it was my birthday. As I proceeded for the door, he called to me and threw an object at me.

I caught it. It was a sergeant chevron. That was how I got promoted to sergeant. My nemesis there was still a corporal. He never quite said anything, but he withdrew from me a little more.

The second greatest moment was when my time was up in this assignment and I had an option to transfer wherever I wanted to go. He called me into his office and helped me to decide on the best assignment for me. I chose Seattle, Washington on independent duty.

There I met and married my first wife. I was twenty-three and she was thirty-three. She was cool and my best friend. We lived together for about two years before getting married. I got injured and surgery forced me to receive a medical discharge from the Marine Corps. I was transferred to Camp Lejeune, North Carolina. There I was discharged and immediately flew back to Seattle the same day. My wife and I rejoiced and partied for a little while, but our fun soon came to an end.

Reality set in when I took home her to meet my mother. You see my wife was as blonde haired and blue eyed as they came. I had already told my mother so she would not be shocked. She said she could handle it, but the combination of my wife's age and her being white was too much for Mom and she let it be known. Knowing my mother as I did, I vowed not to give her the opportunity to express those feelings to my wife. I knew that given the chance she would not hold back and probably hurt my wife's feelings.

Everything seemed to be going well. The three of us were sitting on the living room sofa and conversing comfortably. About ten minutes passed and my mother asked me to get something from the kitchen. I happily got up and walked toward the kitchen. As I exited the living room, I heard my mother begin her speech and before I could return it came out of her mouth.

"I just don't think you are any good for my son."

Damn! That trip was pretty solemn after that and we did not stay as long as we had planned. You see North Carolina was not the place for interracial couples at the time. What I didn't know at the time was that my great-grandmother had been a white woman. Yes, my mother's grandmother was white. My mother's father was Cherokee Indian. My mother grew up with firsthand racism and did not want that for her son. I later came to realize that my mother was just trying to save me some anguish later.

I will interject a short story here that I knew nothing about until I was in my forties and my mother was deceased. Back in high school, there was this girl in one of my classes. We liked each other and talked on the phone quite a bit.

She would call my house and I hers. My mother would tell me sometimes that someone called for me and she said it sounded like a "white girl." I just told her it was a classmate. She warned me not to be messing around with no "white girl" because it was dangerous. Finally this girl and I started to meet secretly and we fell in love or so I thought.

Her girlfriend was dating a different black guy and totally defying her family by seeing him. They were out of control as she would visit his house and his family totally accepted her. Her parents were freaking. Her father sent her away to school and she ran away to come back to her lover. Well, after many threats, this young man was beaten to death and no one really tried to solve the crime, although there was speculation.

What I didn't know at the time was that my mother had received a phone call from a man one night who threatened my life if I didn't stop seeing his daughter. This really upset my mother and as it happened my brother had recently returned from Vietnam. He came in on the night of that phone call and found my mother upset. She told him of the phone call. He was really upset and he returned the man's call.

He explained to the man who he was and that he had just returned home from Vietnam and he was on his way to this man's home.

Well, the man changed his tune and became nicer. However, my little white girl faded out of the picture. I am sure that her father came up with something to keep her in her place. My mother or brother never said a word to me in all that time.

I decided that my wife and I really didn't have much in common and we got an amicable divorce. We did not have any children or create any great portfolio so we did not have much to separate or fight over. My plan was to use my G.I. Bill and continue my college education at the University of Washington. However, since I had begun my college at Columbia College on the Sand Point Navy Base, it was easier to return to school there full time.

Chapter Two

Well, the divorce went as well as one could expect. We just went our separate ways and it was difficult because we saw each other at the places we used to go to together. I would see my ex-wife with other men and feel jealousy and sometimes even anger. She always showed class and I knew she never meant to hurt my feelings. I still have a great deal of respect for her.

I got settled in as a single person and began my pursuit of options from the Veterans Administration. When I went there, a very nice, helpful Asian representative helped me. I remember he made me feel great and I remember thinking, *Wow, the VA really cares about veterans.* Anyway, I got registered for school and my monthly checks began. I was not going to let anything get in the way of my degree. I was not going to work or get caught up in trying to make too much money. I just wanted my degree.

About a week after my visit to the Veterans Administration, I received a phone call from the VA representative that had helped me get started. He asked me to come down to the office for a meeting. I went there the following day and I was offered a job with the Treasury Department. The United States Customs Service had a position for a mail clerk, which could lead to a permanent position as a Special Agent. It was called the Veterans Re-adjustment Act. I accepted the job and started the following week.

I was going to school full time at night and working during the day. It wasn't too difficult a schedule. I was working in downtown Seattle and enjoyed the scenery every day. Some people always complain about the rain, but to me it was always beautiful. I loved Seattle; it was my new home.

In my new position as mail clerk, I lunched at noon everyday. My lunch included a quick sandwich and a walk around the downtown area. One day in a sandwich shop, a well-dressed gentleman approached me. He identified himself as the director of personnel for the Seattle Police Department. He asked me where I worked and asked me if I would be interested in being a police officer. He told me about the salary, which was about two and half times what I was making at the time and had the other benefits. A major consideration for me at the time was that then President Reagan had canceled the Veterans program that I had been hired under. I was stuck in the position as mail clerk with little chance of upward mobility.

I decided to leave the Treasury Department because I saw that I was treated like I didn't belong there. All the people were nice to my face and knew that I deserved a better position, but would not assist me in the process. However, there were several people around me that were promoted and far less qualified. My supervisor even told me when I told him that I was leaving that he knew that I would be better off. He referred to me at U.S. Customs as a square peg in a round hole. He told me I was over-qualified for my position. I realized then the subtle racism within the Treasury Department and decided that leaving wasn't a hard choice.

I gave notice and left for the Seattle Police Academy, which was actually the Washington State Criminal Justice Training Commission.

In my academy class there were about twenty-seven recruits from various departments around the state. There was one other black recruit. He was from a department in Southern Washington. He was former Air Force and he was squared away. We buddied up and we were among the best in our class. We supported each other and we tied at graduation for third in one of the categories. We both knew we were better than that.

One of the things that hurt us was an incident that occurred one night when we decided to party. I took him to a nightclub that I frequented and we got a little drunk. We overslept and were late to the academy the next day. Boy, did we get into trouble. My friend panicked and decided to tell a big lie. I told him that I wouldn't tell on him, but I was going to tell the truth as it pertained to me.

Well, they caught him in his big lie and tried to dismiss him from the academy. They sent him back to his department. He returned a couple of days later because his sheriff pointed out to the mighty Seattle Police Department that they did not set policy for the state academy. He told them he had handled his problem within his department and his recruit would be continuing his training. I received a written reprimand and was allowed to continue.

We graduated and went on to our respective careers within our departments. I contacted him a couple of times, but we didn't stay in touch.

The title of this book was almost "The Crooked Gun."

I discovered that my department issued me a Model 10, .38 caliber police special with a barrel so crooked that it looked like the letter "C". I looked down the barrel and it curved to the left. I immediately told the issuing person in the property room and was told I could exchange it at a later time. Well, when our first qualification came up, I still had the "crooked gun." They had told me they did not have anything better. Thanks to the weapons training that

I had received in the U.S. Marines, I was able to make necessary adjustments and qualify. We called it "Kentucky windage." I had to keep that gun for about six months. The term the "crooked gun" would be relevant to my entire police career.

However, I decided to name this book "Don't Stand Out," because as most blacks know from very early on in life that you have to be twice as good to be equal.

My mother always said, "Do your best always, but try not to show off too much."

Well, when a black man does go out into the world he is the biggest threat to the white man's ego. If you are good, you are arrogant. If you do well on test, you cheated. If you dress nice, you are doing something illegal to afford those clothes. If you are not a drunk, you use other kinds of drugs. If you are not involved with co-workers off duty, you are not a team player. Lastly, if they don't know things about you, they make it up.

The field training phase was my next step. This phase was indoctrination into working the street. Here you spent a month with your first training officer learning to write reports, interview and interrogate people, and learning your way around the district as well as learning different resolutions for a multitude of daily situations.

You observed for the first few days and then your training officer put you out there to handle calls first hand. He stood by if you got in over your head, but it was a time to begin to develop your own style. The goal was not to do it the way your training officer did it, rather it was to get the desired result in your own way.

While on the field training phase, you would get a written evaluation. My first training officer was not very impressive. He was lazy. He did not seem to care if he helped people or not. He used to ask me hypothetical questions constantly about how I would handle blacks in certain situations. It appeared that as a black officer, you must not get a reputation for cutting "brothers" too much slack. The visible other side of that coin was the obvious better treatment of whites in similar situations — more warnings versus citations or arrests.

I handled a few suicides, shootings, burglaries and DOAs (dead on arrivals) or dead bodies that month, but the thing that sticks in my mind at this point more than any other call was the day that I wrote this "brother" three citations in one traffic stop. It was shortly after one of my field training officer's lectures about not cutting brothers slack. We observed a brother riding a motorcycle with out wearing a helmet. This was a no-no. He also ran a stop sign.

So with my excited field training officer at my side, I initiated a traffic stop. I approached the man and he was very cordial, very cooperative and generally a nice guy. The kind of guy that any officer could justify letting off with a warning. Upon further checking with the department of licensing, I discovered that he did not have a motorcycle endorsement. Three offenses, wow, that was a "biggie."

I explained all these offenses to him and he was receptive and accepting of his shortcomings. He was in a tight spot. The motorcycle was his only mode of transportation and he was on his way to a job interview.

The common practice for most officers was to write up the most serious offense, which in this case was the no endorsement, and give warnings for the lesser ones. I informed my field training officer that I wanted to do just that and he said that this was my test and insured that I write the guy for each offense. I wrote the three tickets and then approached the man again. I showed him the tickets and told him I was a rookie and that my field training officer had made me write him up for everything.

He looked at me and he knew that I was in a tight spot. He said, "No breaks today, brother."

This brother was made late for his job interview and probably did not get that job. I have wished many times that I had the opportunity to apologize. I hope he reads my book and allows me that opportunity.

Throughout my next fourteen years, I was careful to always remember that man and treated my brothers with the same courtesy that others received. Ironically, the "crooked gun," appeared on the other side when minutes after writing the brother all of his tickets, we initiated a traffic stop on a nice looking blonde. I don't remember even seeing her infraction, but we stopped her. My field training officer approached her and even called the neighboring patrol car over to see her. They just flirted and gave her a bogus warning. This practice was to become known as "selective enforcement."

After a month with that field training officer, I was moved to a different precinct with another field training officer. I fared a little better this time. He was also an ex-Marine, but after twenty years on the department, he was burnt out. He let me handle things until I needed his help. He didn't seem to have the racial chip on his shoulder.

What I remember as his most redeeming characteristic was his sensitivity. He treated people with professionalism and courtesy. I held on to that throughout my time and it was more in-line with my own philosophy.

In the area that we worked, there were all types of people. Mind you, Seattle is the melting pot of the United States. There are gay people, straight people, lesbians, new wavers, gangsters, traffickers, the wealthy and the poor. There are movie stars and politicians in the area. I have never seen diversity of this magnitude in such a small community.

This field training officer was genuinely a nice guy.

I recall how he would be flagged over by this beautiful transvestite regularly at four a.m. The officer would listen patiently as the would-be woman would rant and rave about how things had changed on the street. After the ranting, he would ask for information about things of concern to officers in the area. If she had information, she would share it with him.

My third field training officer was my wake-up call. Up until this point I had seen a field training officer who was a bit biased, if you will. The second was not as motivated as he could have been. This third guy was a master of the streets. He was not much of a talker, but he was an old-school beat cop. He removed any doubt that I had about who was in control when working the street. He taught me the right of the bat, that you make decisions before anyone else got a chance to. You assessed and acted. Reaction was a bad habit.

He was a man of average stature, but stood very tall. He always looked good in his uniform and was always well groomed. His philosophy was that looking good was fifty percent of the job. If you looked like the authority figure that you represented then people would respect you until you gave them a reason not to. It was therefore not necessary to talk too much.

We would arrive on a call, he would listen if people made their presentation with control and structure. Then he made a decision based on the information he had. His decision was final and everyone knew it. If it were a situation where physical enforcement was necessary, he was prepared for that as well.

I was a black belt martial artist and considered myself able to handle myself, but he showed me the difference between squaring off for a match or fair fight and the kind of fighting necessary for police work. My previous training and the combination of street fighting rounded me a little bit more. I developed more confidence in my ability to communicate, using sensitivity and compassion, while being able to read situations better and foresee the potential for confrontation and immediately exhibit the necessary personality to handle the hostility.

We had day-to-day situations and the lessons came one after the other. I watched one day as he was being harassed by a street type when we were on the main street downtown during the lunch hour. The man finally became too aggressive and assaulted my field training officer. My field training officer was left handed and he hit this man with a left hook that knocked him backward with such force that the man rolled back feet over head and again upright on his feet. The man looked around as if to regain his bearings.

He then walked away in a daze. My field training officer just shrugged and said it wasn't worth pursuing. We didn't see that man in our area again.

For the month that I worked with this field training officer, the other officers in our squad would treat me like a member of the team. They greeted me as "rookie" or "kid" with acceptance. When I was finished with that last month of the field training officer phase, he was to evaluate me and decide if I was ready to hit the streets on my own.

He said that I was ready to go out on my own and get some experience. I was happy and "gung ho." "Gung ho" was a term that we Marines used to describe someone who was highly motivated to get the job done. I was assigned to a one-man car and did not see my field training officer or the old-timers of the squad anymore. Poof! I was solo on the street, which was okay, because I felt people looked at me like I knew what I was doing, ha ha.

Shortly after I was off the field training phase of my rookie training, I was called upon to go undercover. This was again another example of the "crooked gun."

I was not quite sure why I was selected for this assignment because I did not have any prior police experience. I did, however, have experience with weapons from the Marine Corps and my martial arts background. They told me it was because I was a new face in the Seattle area and they could not use known

Seattle officers because of the suspects' knowledge of all of Seattle's black officers.

That still didn't quite excuse the fact that I had not been trained properly nor did I have the required time on the department for such an assignment. This made no sense to me because, as I discovered later, there were undercovers available from federal agencies or other departments. I just thought to myself that I would cover my own backside.

From the beginning of this assignment, I knew something was out of the ordinary. I was told that I was working for a small group of detectives and no one else on the department or in my social life was to know what I was working on. I was to report to work at two a.m. when no other activity was going on in the main building of the department. I only knew the name of the detective in charge of me.

When I reported, I was locked out and had to wait to be admitted. Security, you know, they were all undercover detectives. Most uniform officers didn't know who the undercovers were. It had to be that way because they never knew who they might be investigating.

After a short wait, I was allowed to enter by my requesting officer/detective. He was a nice guy and the group in general consisted of cool dudes, not the stuck-up police types you find in uniform who think their shit doesn't stink.

They began to tell me what types of crimes they investigated and how they proceeded, what type of information was needed and how cases were initiated in undercover units. I could tell this was going to be exciting. It all made sense even if I was an aspiring young rookie.

I was told that I would be investigating some of the more upscale illegal gambling houses. Lots of money and some leading people in the city were involved. As it was explained to me, my job was to figure out how to "bullshit" my way into these establishments and gain the confidence of the people running the activities so that I could identify the people that had had specific jobs — such as who was collecting the bet money, who was running the game, who was cooking and selling the food. The last but most difficult task was to buy alcoholic beverages and identify who sold the drinks to me. After that, I had to collect a sample of the drink in a specimen container that I carried inside my jacket pocket.

I was given three different locations originally and told that no one had been able to successfully gain entrance. The places went by the common name of "after hours."

After the briefing, I was taken to a location away from the department where the undercover police cars were kept. I chose a car and spoke once more with the two detectives that were backing me up. They also gave me a panic pager at that point. The way that worked was once I gained entry into a location they would park close by. If for some reason I got into trouble inside, I pushed the button. The device was fashioned to look like a pager and worked in a similar fashion so as not to appear suspicious. After all was clear, we set out to the first location.

I arrived at the door and saw little activity outside but even the few people that were there seemed nervous. I approached the door anyway. I was very nervous because this was a rough neighborhood and crowd. I knocked and an unknown black female answered the door. There was no light on inside. She asked who I knew and I said that one of the dudes outside said I could get a drink and I pointed to one of the men standing in the street. The woman looked at me again. I know she decided that I was too overdressed to be with that crowd. She wouldn't let me in, so it was on to the next location.

En route to the next location I pulled over so I could explain what had happened. The detectives said that was okay. I drove off to the next location and the detectives followed me. I parked in front of a nice house in the Madison Valley neighborhood. The front porch light was on and several cars were parked in front on both sides of the street. It was about three-thirty a.m.

I got out of my ride and strolled up to the porch. I knocked on the door and waited calmly. The person answering the door was a black man. He was nicely dressed and was quite comfortable with me. He let me in and I went straight into the game room. I watched the game in progress as I waited for my first bourbon and water. I felt a lot more comfortable in this environment as these people were more my style. I made a few acquaintances and was able to get all the information and the alcohol sample that was required.

I had to gamble a bit to be legit to the folks, so I lost about fifty dollars of the city's money. I made a classy exit and was welcomed back any time.

I got back into my ride. This time I felt like I might know what I was doing. It went well. I pulled over and the detectives pulled up behind me. I acted a little dejected, and just when they knew that I had failed, I pulled out the alcohol sample. They were stoked and I felt like "the man." We had a short conference before it was on to the next locale.

Now this final one was a job for the "varsity." I made my way through a couple of people on the porch and knocked. A very nice looking, middle-aged, well-dressed woman answered the door. She was quite officious looking and acting as well.

She asked, "What do you want?"

I told her that "Junior" had sent me. She asked me what my name was. I told her my name was Sam. She looked at me hard and she let me know that she didn't trust me by the way she followed me after she let me inside. I sat down at the card table and took out a handful of money. I had it folded nicely with a few twenties on the outside. The others at the table seemed to appreciate my presence a little more after seeing my roll.

However, there was an older gentleman sitting at the end of the table facing me. You see, the card table was actually a regulation pool table. There were seven people sitting around the table gambling. This old man wasn't playing. He was watching me like a hawk and he never said a word.

I ordered my drink, bourbon and water, of course. I managed to collect my sample and made mental notes as to who was collecting what and their respective jobs. I lost about one hundred dollars there and let it be known that I had to make my departure. The same lady that had let me in followed me to the door. She had not changed her opinion of me. It was obvious that she did not like or trust me.

She opened the door, and as I walked out, she asked again, "Who did you say sent you?"

I told her, "Junior."

She said, "Okay."

I walked away to my car, got in and drove away.

I know she watched me until I was out of sight. I drove around a little bit before I headed back to park the car. The detectives followed and picked me up. After learning about the second success, they were elated. We went back to the office and did the appropriate paperwork as well as placed the samples into evidence. It was about five a.m. at that point and it was time to go home. They gave me a great pep talk, part of which was to inform me that Saturday night, being the next day, would be the test. Friday night had been a tune-up for the big time. I was to report the same time the next day. I left there feeling like I could do the job and that this was the way to start police work. I knew that first night that I was made for undercover work.

Well, as shiny as a brand new penny, I reported at about one-forty-five a.m. on Sunday. I was dressed like a cool dude. They issued me flash cash, gave a smaller gun that was easier to conceal and I surrendered my badge and police identification temporarily. Working undercover, you would not want to get caught with police ID. As for the gun, as long as it did not look like a police weapon, it was cool because everybody had one.

We had our briefing to refresh the rules and clear up any questions. When everything was straight, off we went. We went back to the garage and I picked up the same car that I had used the night before. We decided that we would visit the same places in the same order as the night before. I started with the place where I had been unsuccessful on Friday night.

I parked a few doors down the street. Things were pretty much the same as before with a couple more people hanging around. I gave a short, "What's up?" and tried to look like I had been around before. Then I knocked at the door. The same black female answered the door.

She gave me a hard look and said, "Who did you say sent you?"

I turned around to the group standing close by and said, "Dude," as I pointed to a black dude who nodded in the affirmative.

This female gave me an up and down look and said, "I'm sorry, but I ain't lettin' you in here."

I made a short plea without begging, and said, "Awright den, another time."

I started to walk off and she said, "Hey, you know, bring somebody back that I know and it ain't no problem."

I could see that she was lightening up a little bit, but I had to stay cool, so I said, "I'll do dat."

I left the porch and stopped to chat with the fellas In the street. I asked, "Where da party et?" And jibber-jabbered a bit to make them remember me if I came back around.

I kept my hand in my pocket the whole time because there were some bad-looking actors out in that street. I got out of the area without incident and drove directly to the second house.

Things at this location went basically the same as the night before. I collected my sample and got the information necessary for my reports and left without incident. I did make a couple of friends and was told to come back the next week. This guy was a reputable dude and had a good government job retirement. He had "bucks" and was just supplementing his income.

On to location number three.

Upon my arrival to location number three, I was thinking about how to gain the approval of the skeptical proprietor. I just decided to be cool and play it by ear.

I knocked. She answered the door in much the same manner as the night before. I entered the house and the tension was a little less. I did my thing and got out.

I also received encouragement to return the next week. I believe that was because I won about seventy-five dollars initially, but lost about two hundred dollars before leaving with my sample and my information. I made friends and left.

The investigations went on for about three weeks. The time was extended to see if we could get more information about new locations from the ongoing ones. The first location I had tried closed down or changed locations, probably because I spooked them.

The other two places kept going and so did I. After we had all the evidence we needed, the raids were planned. We had backup in place. There were detectives and uniformed officers standing by.

A lot of tension was in the air when I arrived at the office the night of the planned raids. Everyone involved was present. None of the officers or other detectives knew who I was. I was in another room. They were told that an "undercover" would be inside, but they should treat everyone inside the same until the scenes had been secured.

Everyone left the office and went to the prearranged gathering place. My assigned detectives and I stayed back.

I was given a better panic system and we decided on a signal to "kick the door."

Location One, I arrived in front at about three a.m. on Saturday night. This would be Sunday to normal people. There were several parked cars in front. Everything looked good. The same man let me in and by this time we had become friendly. I went into the game room and ordered my bourbon and water. Then I excused myself to go to the restroom before I started to gamble. There I secured my sample in the container and placed it into my jacket pocket. I then went to the table and exchanged pleasantries with the other patrons that I had become familiar with over the past few weeks. I placed my first bet and received my cards. At that point I pushed the panic button.

As soon as I pushed the button, I placed both of my hands on the table because I knew the door was coming down in seconds. I did not want some over-zealous cop shooting this unidentified black undercover agent. Well, the door came down as scheduled. I, along with everyone else inside, was secured and placed under arrest without incident. My detectives removed me without blowing my cover. The other detectives processed this scene as my team went on to location number two.

Location Two, I arrived in front of the location. There were more people in front than at any time before. This could be bad for the raid team because the more people outside the location and the commotion inside made for chaos. I knocked on the door and the same female answered it as on previous occasions. She was getting a little friendlier each time I came back. This was to be my last visit.

I went in, ordered my drink, and went to the bathroom before trying to win everybody's money. I collected my sample while in the bathroom and prepared to push the panic button. Once back in the card room, I sat at the end of the card (pool) table.

The same older black gentleman who always sat at the other end was there. He never spoke to me; he just sat there and watched the game. His hands were always under the table. A passing thought about this man was that he was always well dressed and wore a nice derby. I put up my money and received my cards.

I studied my cards and subtly pushed the panic button. I again placed my hands on the table and very shortly after that the door came tumbling down. Everyone was secured and placed under arrest.

After the dust settled, I was uncuffed and identified to the other officers. All of a sudden, the black female who had been running the house became irate. She said she had never trusted me and she knew something was wrong with me. She called me a "shit-colored nigger." That was the first time I had been called that. She was really pissed. This lady hated me. The detectives were really pleased with this last location and I didn't quite understand it right away.

We got back to the police station and proceeded to complete the necessary follow-up and I was told that this lady was someone they had been after for a long time, but she was too slick. It turned out that she was a secretary to a city councilman and had connections in the department so she would get information about who might be working on her activity. Her daughter was also a police officer in our department. She had had her own problems with the other side of the law, but was still enforcing the law that others had to abide by.

I discovered that I had been recruited for this assignment because I was unknown to the area. The investigators told me that officers were not willing to work on this woman's case because of her connections.

I didn't appreciate the situation that this put me in for a number of reasons. One reason was that I became a cop to enforce the law for all. Secondly, after the arrest of this woman, the black officers treated me like I was the criminal. Thirdly, the department took me in all my naiveté to do good and used me without explaining until it was over. That was wrong.

I would have done it anyway, but I know the best way to investigate is make sure your undercover has all the information possible. He needs to make good choices based on all known information. In cases of this sort, where you have an undercover with first-hand knowledge, the cases are pretty open and shut.

They must have pleaded guilty, because I was never summoned to court. Because of this assignment, I was pretty much ex-communicated by the black officers for about three years. I was on my own, but I made my reputation as a good cop on my own.

Chapter Three

Oh yeah, I had no idea that woman loved cops like they do. Case in point, we have an annual event in Seattle called Seafair. As I was getting ready for some overtime one night during Seafair, I was dispatched to a minor accident, which turned out to be a major accident with very bad injuries. The woman who created the accident was a nice enough looking woman from an uppity suburb of Seattle. She was oblivious as to her situation as she was only interested in getting the paperwork finished so she could attend the parade.

Anyway she was coming on to me as I was handling the accident and I was not responsive because I was missing my overtime money. I cited her and let her go on her own when I was finished. One thing about her that stood out was that as she was sitting in the back of my patrol car, as is policy, she reached into the front seat, took my soda pop and began to unscrew the cap.

I took my pop back and told her, "I don't know where your mouth has been."

She appeared to take offense, but was quickly over it.

She then made a comment about my wife being upset about me being late getting off.

I said, "Luckily, I am not married."

That was what she wanted to hear. I told her that I would be in the precinct writing reports for hours.

She left. Shortly after I arrived at the precinct and started my reports, I was paged and told that I had a phone call. It was her. I was flattered and agreed to meet her for a drink when I finished my reports. Well, I met her and that started a short affair. She was wild and a lot of fun.

We had a movie date one night and I picked her up and we drove into Seattle. As we drove down a busy street, I saw a man running in the middle of the street.

He was disoriented and bleeding and screaming, "I been robbed!"

I went to his aid and my date said, "Let the police handle this."

I told her, "I am the police."

I decided to impress her when I saw another man running away from the scene. I pursued him in my car with my date. She was excited and didn't know what to expect. Truth be told, when a cop springs into action, he never knows the outcome until it is over. I drove my vehicle in a direction to intercept the suspected perpetrator. I caught him in a parking lot.

We squared off and I drew my weapon. The suspect's reaction to my weapon was one of aloofness. He knew that I had no grounds to shoot him. I did not have enough information and the situation was not a threatening one.

I threw my gun into my vehicle with my date and closed and locked the door. The suspect then walked toward me with a smile on his face. I took a step back and placed a well-timed front snap kick into the suspect's chest. I watched as if in slow motion he doubled over and his posterior seemed to reach for the stars. He left the ground and came down face first onto the pavement. He did not move. I waited until other police officers arrived and took him away. He did not want to fight.

Well, suffice it to say, my date went well that night. As I got more comfortable with my position as a defender of the public (little pun), I discovered that every single day there was an opportunity to meet women. They were everywhere. It was like they felt the way to get good drugs was to get close to a cop. This was very discouraging. I met some very beautiful women but after they realized that I was not into drugs, they left. I would see them at other times with sleazy guys who were "druggies."

I began to visit Vancouver, British Columbia on my weekends. It seemed to be cleaner living over there with even more women. Of course, there were places to go where you could do the things that I wanted to avoid in Seattle, but you had to look for it. Vancouver, to this day, remains one of my favorite places on Earth.

43

During these discoveries about women, I got my first taste of having a partner, an actual day-to-day eight hours with one person. He was a Mexican guy from Texas. He looked black, but don't even mistake him for black. He would quickly correct you if you called him black. Although when it saved his butt to have people in the black community perceiving him as black, he was all too ready to shuck and jive. He had been on about six months longer than I and fancied himself seasoned.

Well, I think common sense had been left out of his repertoire as he complicated everything. He used to report me to my superior for something every opportunity he got.

I must interject at this point that I did not feel that I needed to follow the crowd. I had older brothers that I emulated. The people that I have met out in the world don't impress me as much as my older brothers. I have only ever wanted to make my family proud. This seemed to bother people the more time I had in the department. I truly feel that wherever I am in the world, my first thought is to not do anything to embarrass my family and to always make them proud.

Well, the young cops in the other squads didn't like me much because they thought I thought I was too much. The older cops didn't know that I was alive because I was a rookie. I was in no man's land. I didn't think that I was too much. I was just confident in myself. I think that I appeared over-confident because of the martial arts, but I didn't fear men because of position or stature. I knew that all men put their pants on the same way. You should only give respect when you receive it. It was and is that simple.

This attitude has caused me some grief along the way, but I am satisfied.

My sergeant seemed to like me. He was a former Marine and I know he recruited me because I was a Marine.

Shortly after I was in my new assignment as a solo uniform officer, I got some respect. One day right after we hit the street, I was riding in my one-man car. I was styling and looking good. I heard a call for help. My dilemma was that the call was coming from an old-timer. They didn't normally want rookies anywhere around their calls. I waited for other veterans to answer up and go to his rescue.

You have to understand something; the highest priority call police officers have is to help another officer. After a few seconds with no response, I hit my lights and siren and flew. I arrived and found the old-timer in a fight with two adult males. We subdued them, and once battered and cuffed, they were placed in the rear seat of my police car.

Proudly, I turned to the old-timer and waited for a thanks or something. He said he would meet me at the station. He walked. Mind you, he wouldn't even get into the rookie's police car. I couldn't believe the old goat.

I took the prisoners to the precinct and waited for him to walk. He took his time, and when he walked in, he said he didn't need anymore assistance and sent me on my way. No "thank you" or anything. I hit the street again, pissed.

The next day, I went to roll call and all the old-timers gave me an "atta boy." That was worth a million bucks.

I guess I opened the door for several rookies to join the downtown squad because shortly after me they started to filter in. After two years, I found myself as a training officer. I broke in a few officers that were newer than me. Wow, talk about the blind leading the blind, classic case. To be honest, I don't think the same relationship existed between my rookies and me as did with my field training officers and me, but I did my best to make policemen.

There were a couple of the young officers that came into the downtown precinct after I did. My previous training in the United States Marine Corps taught me that nobody liked kiss-asses. Earn your way with blood, sweat and tears. Kissing ass only made for sore lips and butts. This breed was newer than I. One in particular was a punk. However he was a pet of the chief. He was biracial, but when it was necessary to be black, he was. On the other hand, he preferred the "white" side. He tried to do everything that I was doing.

I just let this go and stayed away from him. When I left, he was a captain. It is funny that the people who moved through positions so rapidly have never really been policeman, but are in positions to second-guess real policeman. Frankly this practice sucks, but is widely the standard.

When you become a cop and you have been around a little while, you decide what your specialty is going to be. If you work hard, you can get the opportunity with a little luck and, of course, some white boy's blessing. I had two areas of interest. The first and easiest for me was narcotics. That would be where I earned a reputation as a good solid cop. Patrol duty was necessary first for all new cops before a permanent special assignment could be earned. Narcotics was an assignment that was reserved for white detectives. They did not do anything, but invent investigations for overtime pay.

I sent a lot of people to jail behind drugs. It was so prevalent. All you had to do was wait or just walk around in a high narcotics area and someone would do something really stupid. The question, "Why do you think they call it dope?" really applies. It may seem really impossible to a person with common sense that a police officer could work narcotics in uniform and in a marked patrol vehicle.

I am going to tell you about some of these geniuses that called themselves drug dealers in the most popular street narcotics area in Seattle. This was my beat —12th Avenue and South Jackson Street.

First, there was a young lady named Deborah. She was well known in the area as a heroin addict. She was one of only a few white people who could hang around in this area and not be beaten, robbed or killed. She was in fact beautiful. Her story was that of rich little white girl from the north end of Seattle. Her family was rich and she got involved with a black man from the south end. He was notorious, as was his family, in the Seattle area; a major drug dealer and street thug. He had her on drugs and all the street people knew not to mess with her. He was not a person people wanted to be on the bad side of.

After I first met her, I tried to talk to her all the time. I told her the typical things cops tell girls like her. She wasn't listening because she wasn't ready to listen. I just knew I was going to find her dead one day.

I stopped seeing her on the street after about a year after I met her. I personally never arrested her, but she had several prior arrests for drugs and prostitution. Then she was no longer around. I found out that he had gone to prison and she just disappeared.

One day after I had made detective, I was walking around downtown Seattle at lunch time. This was about seven or eight years after I first met Deborah. This young, very attractive woman walked up to me and said, "Hello."

I responded with a courtesy and she asked me if I remembered her. I had absolutely no recollection of her. She told me her name and I was shocked. She began to walk with me. She told me how her life had been over the past few years. She had been miserable, but she couldn't change her life. She told me that after her man had gone to prison she went to different cities trying to start over, but she couldn't leave the heroine alone. She told me she remembered the speeches I used to give her and she thought of me sometimes. She told me she was now clean (not using drugs) and had a steady job.

We had an unspoken moment of desire, but left it un-acted upon. I wished her well and she left. I took that as a success.

I used to do all kinds of unbelievable things on the street to get arrests. They were all legal. For example I would park my patrol car around the corner and walk back to the corner wearing coveralls. No one would notice me until I was standing beside a dealer with a handful of drugs. He would be just making sales until I said something clever. The other people standing could only laugh. They called me, "baldy" because I shaved my head.

One of my favorites to arrest was a guy named "Shorty." This guy was sixty-seven years old. He was a stone player. He dressed to kill, wore only "Kangol" caps and alligator shoes. He wore great jewelry. The special thing about

Shorty was that he was the only one in the area with a driver's license. This meant he had a car somewhere, but he would never tell me he had a car. He always said he rode the bus.

Sometimes I would just run around the corner toward him and he would throw his bag of drugs to the ground right in front of me. I would pick it up and take him to jail. I would tell him that I hadn't planned on messing with him until I saw him throw the drugs. Then he would be pissed.

I did little things like all the time and got good arrests.

Shorty had a shyster lawyer who was germ. He fancied himself slick and a drug lawyer. He actually tried to get a judge to throw one of my cases out because it was known that I hated drugs for personal reasons. The judge laughed at him and told him to continue. I won the case.

Afterward the lawyer tried to kid around with me. He had no idea that I thought he was the scum of the earth. He just preyed on these poor black people who paid him felony (too much) money. I just looked at him and walked away.

Two others who stand out in my mind are Paulette and Floyd. Paulette was a harmless junkie, I thought. She just always appeared to be out of it. One day I found her "jonesing" on the street. She needed to get high and she was mean. She assaulted someone in my presence and had a syringe in her hand as well. I arrested her for the first time, and as I searched her, I found open sores all over her body. They were all infected and bleeding. You as a normal person cannot imagine this sight. I got sick right there. I put on rubber gloves and took her to jail. I did not see her around anymore.

Then there was Floyd. He was a character of a different nature. Floyd was not your garden variety criminal. He was a narcoleptic. His drug was Ritalin. He preferred to shoot it up rather than use it like the prescription suggested. He would use up his prescription and look for more on the street. Several times as I was arresting Floyd, he fell asleep during the arrests. It was a crack up.

One day I saw a new face on the corner. He was a well-dressed, successful-looking black man. He was nervous when he saw me. I walked up to him and started chatting. He told me he worked at the local hospital. I told him that I was sure he probably did not know it, but he was in a high narcotics area. He said he was just passing through and waiting for the bus. I said "okay" and I left.

I saw him around more and more and finally I approached him again. He looked a little more worn. He had lost his family, his home, and lastly his job. He started crying and told me he should have listened to me, but before he knew what had happened he was addicted to cocaine. I thought about his nice family, his kids, his wife and his house; now all gone.

The last example of the wonderful world of drugs is about a fourteen-year-old girl. She started out like the others. She just started hanging with some older dude in the neighborhood. She had all the smart-ass answers when I used to question her. Then slowly, as I saw her more and more around, her nose would be running, she would smell bad, wearing the same clothes with wide open eyes. Always going somewhere in a hurry, but never leaving the area.

One night as I was about to get off shift, an informant of mine from the past came up to me at the precinct and told me that that same little girl was the main attraction at a nearby "crack house." He said that she was on a mattress on the floor of the living room. Everyone who came in to buy crack could fuck her for ten dollars. She did not even get the money; she got to get high with the guy that bought her. This informant was really upset and he told me I had to do something.

I was already off duty and could not get any assistance at shift change. So I went to the house and everyone was gone. I felt so helpless because I knew she was there somewhere beyond help. Police work is not all glamorous.

51

I did many investigations throughout my fourteen plus years as a cop. The one that gives me the most satisfaction is about a seven-year-old girl. I can't use any names here, but please give her and her family members names so you will realize that they are real human beings. Give the suspect a name so that you know that we could all know people like this and not know it.

The story starts out like this. I was working the afternoon shift. I hit the street at noon. It was right at shift change and the officers working the morning shift were heading into the station to go home. The new shift was in roll call waiting to hit the street. This was the time when the least amount of officers were on the street. This is no big secret because criminals plan their crimes around this time. I was one of the first to log on and become available for calls.

I immediately received a hot call. It was a call about a seven-year-old who had been molested and the adult suspect was trying to flee the scene. I hit the emergency lights and siren and sped in the direction of the call. This was not in my normal patrol beat and I was a bit far away. Traffic was not that bad and I got there in a short time.

As I drove into the area, radio informed me that the suspect had just driven off in a yellow cab. I had to decide whether to pursue him or contact the victim. As a cop you sometimes get consumed with just getting the bad guy, but the victim was and should be the main concern. Besides the suspect was known and we could get him later.

I contacted the mother of the victim, and after assessing that the situation was under control inside and the suspect was in fact gone, I gave dispatch the suspect's description and advised what he was wearing, driving and possible last direction of travel.

I then sat down with this little, beautiful, sweet, well-mannered girl. Her mother and her younger brother sat in the room with us. She was excited to talk to a real policeman. I could see she felt comfortable with me and was ready to help me. I wanted her know that I was there for her. I slowly began our talk. I can't call this an interview, because it was already personal.

Her mother was very impatient and wanted to get to the topic. I tried to understand her need to vent. I asked the mother how we had gotten to this point. I reassured her that the suspect was being looked for as we spoke. She relaxed and began to speak. She told me that the suspect was her live-in boyfriend of several months. She told me that she worked two jobs and had been at work that morning until around eleven a.m. She said that when she got home the whole family was sitting around in the living room watching TV. An infomercial came on the television about unwanted touching. It informed young children that, if someone touched them in a way that made them uncomfortable or hurt them, they should tell their teacher, parent or a policeman.

The little girl blurted to her mother that the suspect had done that to her. The suspect jumped to his feet in shock and ran to the bedroom. He gathered his belongings.

The mother went into the bedroom because it had not quite sunk in what her daughter had said and she did not know what the suspect was doing or why he was so upset. He said that he had not touched her and then he left in a hurry. That was when I arrived. I then told the mother that I needed to talk to the victim and asked her to let us talk uninterrupted.

Of course, the mother remained present. The little girl was precise about every detail. She told me that the suspect had given her little brother some money and sent him to the store that morning. The store was several blocks away. She said that he then told her he was going to give her a bath.

He put her in the bathtub and washed her as he touched her private parts. She said that he then took her to her bed and got into bed with her. She said that he played with his thing and then he put it inside her privates. She told me that he hurt her. She then told me that this was not the first time this had happened.

The mother broke down and said she had had no idea.

She blamed herself and was just sick. The little boy verified the part about the store and said that that had happened before also. He had never seen anything.

I called my sergeant and explained what I had and told him I wanted to handle this from start to finish. I carefully collected the sheets and towels. I collected items that the suspect had handled that morning as well as some of his personal items. I then took mother, daughter and brother to the hospital.

I contacted social services and explained that I did not think the mother was at fault and that this little girl needed an examination. The mother was inside the examination room with her daughter and I stayed outside with the little boy. I was working on the paperwork and entertaining him.

The nurse came and asked me to come with her. She had tears in her eyes as she told me the little girl had been having intercourse for a while. Her vagina was like that of a sexually active woman. They had collected samples and treated the little girl.

I then took the family home. I stayed and assured them that this case would be handled right and this man was going to jail for long time. I left and put the evidence into the evidence section.

I followed up daily and the suspect was caught and the case was tight. He got twenty-five years.

I received a letter of his continued incarceration from the Department of Corrections once a year because they knew I had a continued interest in this case. The family moved out of that neighborhood and I did not see them anymore. I never forgot them and I still feel good about that case.

About a year after that case, I investigated a young man assaulting an elderly man at a downtown bus stop. I responded and observed the young man pushing the older gentleman around and taking his belongings.

I drove up to them and the young man was quite belligerent. I returned the gentleman's items to him and he got on the bus. The young man became more unruly and finally I decided to arrest him.

He pushed me and tried to run away. I caught him and he punched me. At that point I used a take-down technique and put him on the sidewalk. He received a minor cut to his head. I took him to the hospital for stitches. It was then that he informed me that his father was a cop.

I had not done anything wrong, but another cop's kid could always be a problem. I called my lieutenant and told him the situation.

I was not quite sure how the Lieutenant would react. If you remember the incident that I had in the academy, well, the lieutenant had been the sergeant in charge of training at the time. I did not think he liked me very much.

So when the hospital was finished, I called the young man's father and explained that I had had to arrest his son. I also told him that I had used force in the arrest but his son was all right.

I told him that we were leaving the hospital and would be in the precinct shortly. There I would release his son to him as a courtesy. He became very upset with me and threatened to get to bottom of this.

When he arrived at the station, my lieutenant met him and jumped on his case about his son's attitude toward police officers. He further told him that his son was lucky because he could have really been hurt.

My lieutenant then called me forward and introduced me to the officer. The man apologized and took his son home.

It turned out that the young man was the best friend of the suspect that I had sent away for sexually abusing the seven-year-old little girl in the case I mentioned earlier.

Years later, after I had made detective and wore suits every day, I went into my dry cleaners to pick up some clothes. The owner was the godmother of that young girl and she told me that the girl was now eighteen and worked there. She arranged for us to meet again.

It was good to see her all grown up, but I still cried for her. I swear to God, sometimes I don't how I lasted fourteen years as a cop. It just seemed like everything made me cry.

Chapter Four

Up until this point I had had partners that were only temporary. But now it was time to get to know the first guy that would become my "think-a-like." He was a Japanese officer, a likable guy. He was of upper class upbringing and had gone to one of the popular colleges in the state of Washington. He was a little "yuppie" police officer.

He had no interest in the plight of the people he served.

He didn't have to.

All during our shifts, he would concern himself with not letting his Rolex get damaged or his uniform mussed. Now my uniforms were my pride as well as expensive, but I was a cop and cops got dirty sometimes.

People call the police when they need help. Most of the time it is when they are not at their best. This guy didn't care what their problems were, he wasn't there to resolve anything, and he would just take reports. This was how you covered your ass.

Working downtown Seattle was an action beat. As a two-man patrol car, we got our share of it. Each squad had at least one two-man car. They were the action cars. If something needed immediate attention, they sent the two-man car. When you worked the two-man downtown, sometimes you got to go "hands on." This boy didn't like to do that.

The problem with that attitude was that people on the street were watching you. The "bad guys" learned what cops were "chumps" and which ones they could play with. It was very easy to be made a fool of on the street by street types. So as a newer officer, you couldn't get pulled into their games. You wouldn't live it down.

This officer was a punk. I am sorry, it is true. He never cared if he served the public; he worried about Wall Street or his other investments. He and his little wife had the BMWs and a nice house in a better neighborhood — set up originally by his father, of course. After a few months together, my sergeant called me aside and told me to watch my back because my partner was saying that I was too aggressive. My sergeant liked my work and told me that he thought that I should know what he was saying.

I appreciated being told, but it didn't change anything because I knew I was doing my job right. If I could resolve a situation by making an arrest, I did. If I needed to remove someone from a premise without the arrest, I did.

DON'T STAND OUT!!!

If I could pay for a hungry shoplifter's food, I did. I enjoyed my job and the challenge of affecting people's lives positively. At the end of my days, even early in my career, I used to evaluate how many people I had influenced positively each day. I was developing into a good cop.

This partner was also in the little "clique" and heard about the good things people were saying about me. He didn't like that and said that he wanted to work a one-man car. I was very glad to accommodate this. My sergeant liked me in a two-man car and trusted my police work. He paired me up with another Mexican officer. He was a good guy and we got along fine. We were friends for about one and half years off and on duty.

As I got to know him, I discovered that he had some characteristics that were not redeeming. I also felt that he was trying to set me up. His activities outside work were suspect and I stopped socializing with him. He sensed my discomfort with him and distanced himself. Last I heard he had been promoted. That figured because there was also a convicted rapist on the department as well as other criminals in uniforms.

I was seeing major changes in the squad where I had been working. Most of the old timers were retiring and the newer ones in the squad were guys who tried to be like the old timers, but didn't have the character. They dressed sloppily in their uniforms. They drank on duty and took whatever they could get for free.

61

This reminds of another time when I felt that I was being set up. I had just been given a new beat. It was on the waterfront. If you ask any old timer about days gone by, they would tell you that this was a prime beat to have — lots of perks, if you know what I mean. Well, my first day on this new beat that I wasn't sure I wanted, and didn't understand how an officer with so little time on the department could get, I went to a restaurant. A senior officer had recommended this restaurant.

I walked inside and sat down. I was approached by a waitress who was a "hash slinging mama." She had been waiting on cops since the turn of the century. She wanted me to accept my meal without paying. I refused and left in a hurry and did not return. I gave up that beat.

Another one of my partner's friends made captain. These were guys that the dirt would eventually come out on or they would be controlled by local politics. I didn't take too well to the cliques around the department. Thus started my first brush with department politics. The "crooked gun" popped up again.

In 1985 I was given a thirty-day trial period to join the SWAT team. This was a group of guys that were supposed to be the elite of the department. They were, however, just guys who were using this position to make lots of overtime. Everything, I was learning, was to "justify your existence."

When I reported my first night for roll call, they were sitting around like a group of good ole boys.

They made a few comments that were, let us say, not in good taste.

I was told that, "You have got to have thick skin in this outfit."

It was simply to see if I would go along with their redneck ways. I maintained. I was to work with a different officer every night and be evaluated — not only my police work, but my ability to work as a team member. This part I understood, as it was important to be a team player in potentially high-pressure incidents. I got along well with the other boys and I was voted in. The opening was not immediately available, so I was to go back to my patrol until the opening occurred, which would be in about two months.

I went back to my day squad as a patrol officer and a field-training officer. I was enrolled in college and I was also a member of a martial arts school that took up a lot of my time. I went to my sergeant and requested that I be allowed to change shifts to accommodate my schedule. It was a good move for all involved because the morning shift was short of officers. This shift was from three a.m. to eleven a.m. It was a hard shift because of the hours.

I was assigned as requested. My lieutenant was also a friend and everything was done without any paper trail. It wasn't necessary. It was also good practice to keep your name out of departmental print as much as possible.

Well, everything was set and I reported as ordered along with my new rookie. I knew the new sergeant and he called my name. I answered that I was present.

The new lieutenant responded, "Who the hell are you?"

I looked at him and chose not to respond to his disrespectful inquiry. The lieutenant was a large man, fat and tall actually. He was a loud person and quite obnoxious. He was a bully. I have always hated bullies.

I have been considered arrogant and pompous by many that have met me, but I consider myself confident and capable.

Not getting the response he wanted from me, the lieutenant simply took the copy of the roster with my name on it and shouted he would get to the bottom of this. I took my new rookie and we hit the street.

Once in the car, my rookie asked me what that was all about. I didn't respond, but thought, *Nice first impression of the department for a rookie.*

We went on with our business of "protecting and serving."

The sergeant in this new squad was a black veteran cop. I thought at least there would be some kind of camaraderie, not special treatment, but acknowledgment that blacks universally share. This would be my first experience with this "cheese eater," but not my last. The lieutenant took my attitude toward him as non-compliance and took me on as a challenge. He would put me in my arrogant place.

Between the sergeant and the lieutenant, I was not given certain rules of the squad and information that I should have had. I could not play by the rules if I didn't know them. So when I made sufficient mistakes, I was referred to the captain for discipline. This put me, the lieutenant, and the captain in the office for this event.

I was silent as the lieutenant spoke about my bad attitude and incompetence.

When he was finished, the captain allowed me to speak. I was candid and spoke freely about the lieutenant's treatment of me and his bad attitude as well. I repeated some of his words and actions in the presence of others and he became incensed. He rose from his chair and approached me. I rose from my chair and met him.

I took a defensive stance as I was sure he was upset enough to attempt to assault me. He saw no fear in me and, puzzled, he withdrew his person from my face and continued his hostilities verbally.

The captain then asked me to leave the office. I did. From outside I heard the captain give the lieutenant the "what for." The lieutenant exited and the captain asked me back inside.

Once inside, he told me to continue as before and I would have no further problems with the lieutenant. The problems did continue, but I handled them without involving the captain. This bothered him more than any other method that I could have handled the situation with. I ignored him, the worse thing you can do to a man with a testosterone problem.

Time was passing and I was getting closer to the date of my transfer to SWAT. One day the lieutenant overheard someone speak of my transfer and he said, "I'll see about that."

The lieutenant went to the lieutenant of the SWAT team and told him about my inherent bad attitude and basically told him that I didn't have his approval for transfer. I was so notified and my subsequent transfer was canceled. I even had it in writing. Just like that, no SWAT team transfer, the "crooked gun" again.

I was, to say the least, upset. I protested to my captain and some others who would listen. They could only offer me a consolation prize. This was supposed to be a shit assignment. I was going to turn it into a gem of a position.

Chapter Five

The department had decided to start a new unit. It was to be the official start of the Seattle Police Department's Street Narcotics Team. I was asked if I would be interested in a position on this team. There would be four officers who had shown initiative in the area of narcotics and undercover work. My prior work in undercover had already convinced me that I would like this assignment. I accepted the job.

We were briefed as to what would be expected of us and given room to develop standard operation procedures for narcotics agents. We were under the guidance of a detective with lots of narcotics experience. He had made some big deal years ago and was still riding high on that ancient case.

He was a burn out. He was flash and cash, wore gold and played the player on the city's account. He spent lots of the city's money and worked no cases.

The four officers selected were good officers. The first was a female with about five years as a patrol officer. She was respected and had no interest in undercover. She made that clear. She also understood that this was going to be the unit to be in for career advancement. This was because everybody and their brothers were on the "get tough on drugs" bandwagon. We actually became friendly. She used to tell me a little about the details of her private life. She was always choosing the wrong man.

This was interesting to me because I had been the wrong man for many women up until that point. I learned that I was not the wonderful man that I thought I was in a relationship. I learned a lot from her. I actually became a sensitive man and really discovered how to be what women wanted. I must confess that at times I played with my new discoveries just to test them. So you see, she was a good, well-rounded cop who didn't take herself too seriously. She was assigned and did a good job in a backup role.

The second officer was a guy that I had worked around in patrol. He considered himself a narcotics specialist. He used to make narcotics arrests frequently. His reports used to make interesting reading. How he could see from blocks away and readily identify the different types of illegal substances as they passed hand to hand in quantities the size of match heads was amazing. He knew he was going to shine in this new unit. The reality turned out to be that he couldn't buy marijuana from a pharmacist if he had a prescription.

You see, the makeup of the neighborhood that this second officer worked in and scored his numerous narcotics arrests in was predominantly African-American. And why is this an issue? Well, glad I asked myself that question.

When people think of Seattle, they think of this very liberal city, the melting pot, if you will. However, the police department was still biased, as are many modern-day departments. Essentially these arrests would never have been signed off on by supervisors if they had occurred in other parts of the city. Lacking in resources, the recipients of this particular brand of justice did not have the means to fight back. So with the help of court appointed attorneys, they would find themselves pleading guilty to felonies, gross misdemeanors and misdemeanors and considered themselves lucky to get a few days in jail. They never thought that they were railroaded and now had felony convictions that would follow them forever.

Job applications are not that attractive with felony or misdemeanor convictions on them. This is something I will discuss at length later.

The third officer was a little, short, fat Mexican. He was a six-or seven-year veteran. He really saw himself as macho and cool. In actuality he turned out to be quite an undercover. He had guts that I never expected and street smarts that had been undetectable before this assignment.

He also worked his patrol years in an African-American community.

Although not as blatant as idiot number one, he also had no regard for African-Americans. You see, one of the things I have learned about police work and the judicial system in general, is that there are two sets of rules. Now mind you, the system would be right out in front telling you that the poor little blacks were just "junkies, thieves, liars, pick your crime, they are all into it." That was what they would have you believe. The thing about this accepted farce is that they have been able to sell this to the world.

When I travel abroad, people are so surprised at how different blacks are in real life compared to the propaganda conveyed via white media. I enjoy destroying this misinformation personally and challenge all African-Americans to do likewise every time they get the opportunity.

One thing about this Mexican American police officer as with many American ethnicities, they try so hard to be part of the great white machine that they give themselves away, never realizing that when the machine is through using them, they will be discarded. He hung himself out there buying into the mystique that surrounded the undercover officer.

It was an exciting lifestyle, the fast lane with no consequences. This was what an undercover thought if he didn't keep himself in check. I could tell when this officer compromised himself. He changed one day. I saw him as someone who had given away his soul.

One of my brothers used to say, "When a man loses his character, he never gets it back."

After a couple of years in narcotics, he looked sad to me.

Well, I was the fourth officer. I was very naive and thought that the city trusted me to do a great service. They trusted me to spend their money, make good arrests, and use good judgment. I really enjoyed this job. I think I was too good at it. I could tell that there were some officers who possibly thought I was using or dirty in some other way.

The truth is never. I bought dope from blacks, whites, and Asians, whoever was selling, I was buying.

This unit was started as a result of the "rock house" craze. The California street gangs had moved into the Seattle area and were changing the way the drug business was operated in Seattle. They were ruthless but organized. They weren't as street dumb as we were used to. These guys and girls were smart. They drove very nice cars and dressed in expensive clothes. They were extremely nice to the police when stopped and had all the right answers. They didn't bring unwanted attention to themselves. They were very mobile and were not afraid to do business without limits, definitely not Seattle style.

I moved about a bit in this undercover capacity and got to know a few of the Californians, but you couldn't ask too many questions about them. I tried to inform our intelligence unit about the influx of the gangs and they replied, "We don't have gangs in Seattle."

They are still paying for that stupidity.

The Mexican officer and I were the only ones having success on the streets. We began to work together on several cases and were a good team. About the time we started to jell as a team, the female officer decided to transfer out. Another female came into the squad. She was an ambitious bitch. She quickly

71

assessed that the Mexican officer and I were the two producers. As I thought she was a pig, I didn't have much time for her, anyway I could see straight through her. My partner didn't fair so well.

She quickly seduced him and broke up our partnership. She rode on his shirttails and he in turn was able to pass the sergeant's exam, a good trade. I was not interested in anything but doing what I was doing, being a good "narc." She was promoted and transferred to another unit. The Mexican officer and I never really worked together again; we backed each other up every once in awhile, that's all.

I made my own way and got back-up for my cases from various sources. I made good cases and learned many things from other agencies that I worked with. During this time, I worked with the FBI, DEA, FDA, ATF and various other police agencies. After about two years in narcotics, I was ready for a change. I knew that because suddenly one day I was going about business as usual, following up on a complaint in an affluent area of town. Not really expecting success I casually approached a man who was doing nothing. He was in the doorway of a nice apartment building and I asked him if he knew some guy. I made up a name. He went on to ask me more about the guy.

After about fifteen minutes, I told him that I was looking to buy some cocaine from the guy I was looking for. It just so happened that this guy was there to sell some cocaine. So I bought an ounce of almost pure "flake" cocaine from a stranger in about twenty-five minutes. Here I was on a solo assignment not expecting to buy anything, all of a sudden, bam!

I was excited at my quick thinking and ability to invent circumstances. I decided to not arrest the man and to set up further buys and eventually get a bigger fish. So as I drove back to headquarters to write my report and place my ounce of "quality" cocaine into evidence, it dawned on me that that had been too easy. I was then in the office alone packaging the coke when it dawned on me that someone was testing me or setting me up.

I didn't like being set up or tested. I placed my evidence in the property room and completed my paperwork. Then I went home. I stayed there for about a week. I didn't tell anyone, but I had quit. I only didn't know if I quit narcotics or quit the department. Truth be told, and this is first time I openly say this, I did not trust the cops that I worked with anymore. It occurred to me that this last buy was a setup to check me out.

On another occasion, we received word in the office one day about a very big deal going down. It involved high rollers from South America bringing in a large amount of cocaine. It involved several locations around town and everyone in our office was put on this case. I was assigned as part of the cover team on the local suspect's apartment in Seattle.

This was a very organized investigation. All the raids were to be served at the same time throughout the city. The suspect and his foreign companion were leaving the apartment when our team served our warrant. We detained them and our supervisor was totally apologetic as we found no drugs. I had remained outside during the search of the apartment, but as we were about to leave, I walked inside and looked around. They had left the apartment just as they had found it.

I have seen many raids and, believe me, when they raid black people's places, they destroy everything. They dump all the food from cupboards and the refrigerator. They turn over all the furniture, flip mattresses, cut up carpet, just make a mess. This place was seemingly untouched. I got pissed off about that and began my own search. Mind you, there was a lieutenant and sergeant and another senior detective present.

They looked at me like I was crazy as I walked through the place flipping furniture. I walked into the kitchen and ripped the screen from the ventilation duct above the stove. There I discovered two bricks of pure, high quality cocaine. Everyone ran inside when they heard the thump as it fell onto the stove. All the searchers were embarrassed that they had missed it and played down my success.

This was typical of the white officers' willingness to not get the job done if it involved a black officer getting credit. I don't like to sound like I am super cop, but I think black officers bring a lot to police work and should be acknowledged for it.

Finally after about a week at home, my phone rang. It was my captain. He asked me what was wrong. I told him I was through with narcotics. He asked where I wanted to be reassigned. I told him that I wanted to go to patrol, east precinct. He immediately reassigned me. I left narcotics on excellent terms with a good reputation.

On my first day back, I sat in roll call. The sergeant was an old-time veteran and a friend from my first days on the department. I looked around the room and didn't recognize anyone in that room full of rookies. They all looked at me like I was a rookie and they had no idea who I was. I decided I would re-adopt my attitude from my days in patrol before. "A felony a day, keeps the sergeant away." I would make at least one felony arrest a day.

The rookies quickly discovered who I was. When the sergeant called out my name and serial number at roll call, the rookies knew that I had been around for a while. A callout from the rear of the room informed the sergeant that I had been requested as a partner for the day. I looked around and found it to be another old-time friend. This one was a female officer who had been around longer than I had. She had been nice to me when I was new and knew of my work to date. I was honored that she wanted to work with me.

We hit the street, a two-person car. We got re-acquainted and were driving around the central area. She was driving and I was the passenger officer, which meant that I was to write whatever reports were necessary. After about an hour as we passed down a back street, I observed a young black man walking down the street. He had been to the local grocery store and was carrying provisions to prepare a nice breakfast. I asked my partner to pull over to the curb and I informed her that I was going to arrest the man.

She was shocked and said, "For what?"

I didn't answer. She pulled over and we got out of the car. I greeted the young man pleasantly and he was cordial. We chatted a bit, you know, small talk. After about five minutes, I asked him if he knew me and he said that I looked familiar to him. I laughed and asked if he remembered an incident that occurred in his house about two months before in which a man came by to buy rock cocaine. One of the other customers had recognized this particular customer as a police officer and the officer had to flee out of a window because the man selling the coke pointed a shiny .357 magnum at the officer.

At this point the young man looked at me again and smiled.

"Yes," I said, "I was that cop and you sold me dope."

The probable cause was still good and he didn't get to cook that nice breakfast that morning. I remember thinking how nice and pleasant that young man was that morning versus the cold drug dealer who wanted to shoot me two months earlier. This young man was a prime example of how Seattle had changed in the drug trade.

A year before, the dope peddlers in Seattle were slick enough, but played a milder game. If they got busted, they dealt with it. It was a part of the game, but now these kids would try to kill you instead of losing money. Yep, it was all about money. They were no longer innocent Seattleites; they had been run over by California gang bangers.

As I had much information about these California bangers, the department was still in denial. They would not even address the possibility of gangs. I was still collecting my information on them and saving it. I knew most of them. The department had another idea. They were going to make two little, fair, white boy policemen their gang experts. These two were a joke. They gave themselves street names like the bangers and ran around trying to learn the lingo. It was a joke.

The department even put themselves in the national spotlight when they put these little idiots on a national television show. I was so embarrassed. Gangs at this point were a national problem and the liberal Seattle police department did not want give any black officers the courtesy or respect to know their own culture. I say that to say this. This gang culture was nothing new. As black Americans, we grew up with all types in our communities. We knew who to stay away from. We knew who was doing what in our neighborhoods. Why? Because we all lived in the same neighborhoods at that time. The Seattle police department would rather risk this type of ignorance than acknowledge that blacks could offer an area of expertise. So the department in all its glory put several inexperienced officers in a squad and called them a gang squad.

They wanted me to go into that squad. I declined. It was a smoke screen and a political Band-Aid. Truth be told, I was better than that. My going into that unit would give them credibility. I was and always had been a real policeman. So I chose to go back to patrol in uniform where I could do some good.

The homicide robbery unit fancied themselves the elite of the department. There were some younger officers in homicide robbery that were of my era. They had not had nearly the success that I enjoyed as a patrolman. I looked at them as younger versions of the good ole boy network. They knew they were not better cops, just whiter.

One particular incident that reminds me of their incompetence is as follows. I was flagged down by a lady one day while on patrol. She told me of the homicide of her father a day before and that her brother was the suspect.

He was an adult male and he was on crack. She told me the detectives had been there and done their investigation.

She told me they had not found a murder weapon. The apparent weapon used was a knife. Well, she had flagged me down to tell me that she had found a knife.

I went inside the house and recovered the knife. I called the detective in charge of the investigation. He was at home and he told me that they had searched the house and there was nothing there. He said that I did not need to do anything with that knife. I told him that I would place the knife into evidence anyway. Well, a couple of days later he called me and asked if I could write up a statement. He hated to tell me that it was indeed the murder weapon. I acted stupid, as I knew he hated every minute that I was in his office because he knew I thought he was a fool.

That was how the guys in those units were. They couldn't open their minds and it was reflected in the amount of cooperation between them and other units in the department.

Another example, one night I was dispatched to a possible suicide. When I arrived at the scene as the first responder, I realized that, first of all, this was a known drug address. Then several people were outside and knew the suspect by name. They directed me to him. They were all calm and exact about their story. They told me that the victim had shot himself.

When I walked into the apartment, there were no signs of struggle. I found the victim on the bedroom floor. He was not dead. He was doing still doing "the chicken." There was a handgun in his right hand, but it was positioned in such a way that he could not possibly have shot himself on the left side of his head.

I called for homicide and they reluctantly responded.

I explained what I found upon my arrival. They appeared put off with me and disregarded what I said. They said it was an obvious suicide. I laughed and turned the scene over to them. I left the scene and went home. My shift was over.

It turned out to be a homicide.

One of the biggest problems with law enforcement for blacks is their unwillingness to be black. They can use the quota system to get promoted and complain when they don't get something. Most won't stand up for black citizens who have been mistreated by the department. They stand by and watch other black officers get set up and mistreated and they do nothing. They are afraid of their own shadows and especially the good ole boy network. They don't want to make a difference; they only want to get a pension.

It is a shame. I say again, shame on you.

One officer put it to me this way. The blacks do nothing about the situation because they suffer from the "illusion of inclusion."

He had a very radical demeanor and appeared militant. He was an educated man and spoke of his accomplishments regularly. He was, however, married to a white woman and lived his suburban life.

Chapter Six

The Crips and Bloods were battling over the streets of Seattle. They showed no respect for the locals. The kids from Seattle were taking beatings every day on the street and were afraid to walk around in their own neighborhoods. So they organized and started a branch of the Black Gangster Disciples. This was an old-time gang from the Chicago area. One of the locals had contacts from Chicago and the Seattle group was given the go-ahead.

It seemed like overnight, but the BGDs were cold and mean. They were no longer the "just sell enough to buy forties" teenagers — "forties" referring to the popular beer size of forty ounces. They were about making money right now and taking back their streets. There were shootings, robberies, burglaries, etc., every day. Black kids dying in the streets and the lack of action by the authorities, courts, and the communities showed how much they cared.

I became upset with this attitude and started my own intelligence gathering. I wanted to know who the players were. The department ignored my efforts and decided to appoint two young white rookies as the Seattle police experts. They didn't know shit. They would come to me for information, but were careful not to let anyone know where their information came from. It was a joke.

I would see these chumps on national television programs. They were so stupid; they even gave themselves tags. They ran around like they thought they were "Batman and Robin." It was pathetic.

Then the gang unit was started. I was offered a position there, but it was only to recognize me as second to the "experts." Initially, I declined the spot. Then I was sent there on a thirty-day trial period. I finished the temporary assignment and then again turned down the spot. It was a "colored officer's" position. There were several black and Asian officers in the unit. The Asian gangs were picking up their activity as well by then. The problem was that the Seattle Police Department wanted white officers to appear to be running the show. It was a good example of the mentality of the department. It was just like when I worked undercover in narcotics. They thought they could just take any black officer and send them into the black community and they could buy dope. It was ridiculous and this was the police department. Who were the real dummies?

Black drug dealers were especially careful of blacks they did not recognize. So you had to have some sense of blackness to buy anything from a real drug dealer. Needless to say, not too many black officers could get into these places and even less could present themselves as users or players of the game. That didn't include the ones that were just too damn scared to go into these places without a badge.

Trust me, being a successful undercover is an art. There is a major difference between an undercover and a plain-clothes officer. The public doesn't know that until it is too late. It again reminds me of the martial arts.

You see, I hold a fourth degree black belt in TaeKwonDo.

I have practiced for most of my life. Whenever someone discovers that I am a martial artist, I quickly learn that most people want to impress me with the fact they took some form of martial arts for awhile, but they don't remember what belt they were or the style they took.

The gang bangers ran these idiots around in circles. The department used these experts to show that the situation was under control. They later promoted these boys to real detectives and they filled positions that real cops could and should have had. That was the way the police department operated. The positions that officers work for were given to the undeserving and then real cops became frustrated and stopped trying so hard. They are referred to as "burn outs."

One day as I was on patrol in the central area, at about five p.m. an emergency call came over the radio. There had just been a shooting about four blocks from where I was sitting in my patrol car. As most cops know when a "hot" call comes out, every officer gets there as soon as possible. There was like this unspoken need to kick some butt or shoot someone.

I headed toward the address given. I had received the description of the suspect who had fired into a moving vehicle right in the middle of BGD (Black Gangsta Disciples-ville.) A description of the suspect's clothing was given and a direction of travel. He was on foot. I assessed the situation and knowing the area, I moved south. I saw a man fitting the description hurriedly leaving the area. I saw him before he saw me.

I exited my vehicle, drew my weapon, and steadied my aim at the suspect. I then called out to the suspect to "freeze." He looked toward me in a state of shock. He hands were behind his back. I commanded him to show me his hands. He would not. I yelled over and over as I prepared to fire. I cocked my weapon and waited for his next move.

I recognized the suspect from many contacts before. Prior to this, he had been a petty thief and drug user. That day, he had graduated to homicide.

He thought to run. He thought to fire upon me. I could see his mind racing through his eyes. The situation slowed and the suspect dropped an object to the ground while his hands were still behind his back. He then produced his hands and they were empty. I placed the suspect under arrest without incident.

After taking control of him, my back-up officer arrived and I advised him where the object had been dropped. He picked up the .45 caliber semi-automatic handgun. It was the murder weapon. That was all he did and he received a commendation.

The victim was a seventeen-year-old kid from the neighborhood. He was not a gang banger, he was in a car with some of his friends, who were in a gang, and they were fired upon as they drove down the street. Another terrible thing about this incident was that the kids in the car with the victim drove him straight to Providence Hospital emergency room. The medical staff there looked at him and said there was nothing they could do. They called an ambulance to take him to Harborview Medical Center.

I remember responding to Providence and inquiring about the victim. The attitude was that it was just another black kid and they told me he went to HMC. I went on to HMC and began my reports about the incident. I was in the emergency room watching the staff work on this kid. His brains were blown out. Some pieces were still in the car, some were in the ambulance. He was not going to make it.

When he expired, I sat there thinking, *What a waste.* Then I was informed that his family was in the waiting room. I had to tell them what had happened and then stand by while the doctor told them that he had died from his injuries. It was awful.

A thought crossed my mind while I was contemplating this useless loss of life. It seemed that society was so much more ready to accept the loss of black lives, regardless of the circumstances, than white lives. I began to think more every day that I was working for a system that had no respect for my people or me. I was being used to police my own people. Whites were getting away with the things I arrested blacks for. I would arrest whites, but I would never be subpoenaed to court for the whites.

That takes me back to another situation when I was in narcotics. I was given free reign to investigate drug cases all over the city. As long as I was working on blacks, I was backed all the way. When I was working on whites, I was pulled off cases to assist in other investigations.

Once I was working a big dealer in a prestigious neighborhood. The dealer was the owner of a big company and I received the tip anonymously. I was told I could investigate.

I surprised my supervisors when I made contact with the suspect and bought cocaine from him on two different occasions. I was ready to serve a search warrant on this man when I was taken off the case and it was never followed up on.

It was another case of disillusionment. They just did not want a black officer to receive credit for taking down a big time white dealer. I was losing faith in the system and it would continue. I started to feel like it didn't matter how good a cop I was I was still perceived as a sellout. As far as the white cops went, they would never give me my due. The black cops always held a grudge because of my earlier bust of one of their own.

One night there was a large disturbance at a neighborhood high school playground. Several officers responded. The young experts were there and missed all the indicators of the real problem. I listened to the gang bangers bullshit the experts and make them look like fools. The experts never got it. They thought they had gotten all the details and resolved the matter.

When they finished, I addressed the group of gang members and let them know that I was not so stupid. One thing that the experts let get past them was that this group was a new group from California and they were a bit older than normal. They were really hardcore. They were Santana Block Crips This was a particularly bad sect. They were known for "enforcing." I got into an argument with the leader and we agreed to even out and get physical.

He gave the typical, "Get rid of that badge and we can get it on."

I did and the usual happened; nothing.

The whole thing about this gang shit was no mystery to me. I speak for myself and won't try to speak for any other black on this topic. I grew up in a good black environment. There were gangs around all over the city. There were some really bad dudes in my neighborhood. I was lucky I had four elder brothers and they were known. All someone ever had to say was that was "Sweetpea's" little brother. The nature of the village is that there is always a power structure. This is true even in the white community but for blacks they called us "gangs." The biggest gang there is; is the police, that's right.

Not too long after the killing of the young man previously mentioned, I was dispatched to a call about a suicidal young woman. She had escaped the mental ward at a local mental patient facility. She was holding the staff at bay with a large knife in the kitchen. Mind you, Seattle thinks itself to be a very liberal city. As I was the first officer to arrive, I was directed to the kitchen. There was a group of staff members standing in the doorway watching the patient. There were at least seven of them.

I walked in and asked them to leave. They were hesitant to do so. I asked again with authority and allowed the supervisor to remain. The idea was to get control of the situation. I entered the kitchen and begin to speak to the patient, who was a white female, about twenty-five years old. She was blonde and, although attractive, she was obviously deranged. She would respond to me, and when I tried to get closer, she would put the large kitchen knife to her neck and begin a cutting motion. So I backed off a little.

At this point, other officers arrived and did the typical police thing. They drew their weapons and were ready to fire. They were all standing behind me and threatening the patient. I turned and strongly verbalized my dissatisfaction with their actions.

I asked the two idiot cops, who were standing there weapons drawn and shaking, "What are you going to do, shoot a suicidal person threatening only herself?"

They looked at each other in total stupidity and holstered their weapons. By the way, they were both sergeants when I left.

I again approached the patient and she again threatened her demise. She began to cut her neck, and upon seeing the first red trickle, I drew my baton and raced toward the patient. I grabbed a metal serving tray and held it between us in case she turned the knife on me as I struck her with a full blow across her arm. The knife fell to the floor and I was able to subdue the patient.

Shock at my action was all over the faces of everyone. But in a short moment afterward, everyone realized that I had resolved it in the best possible way. No one was dead. There was minimal injury to the patient's arm and the facility staff was happy.

When I received a commendation for this incident, the inclusion of the "would-be shooters" was a sore spot. It was becoming obvious that I was not to receive any solo credit for my work. Black officers had a history of not expecting to be as good as white officers, even in their own communities. The officers that were good and the public trusted the department took as a threat and found ways to discredit them or transfer them with some of that department bullshit. They had ways to get some type of dirt on most officers to control them, and if that didn't work, just spread rumors about them.

Now, the sergeant changed and the new one was one of the good ole boys. He did not like the fact that the younger officers looked up to me for guidance and leadership. I was happy to help them. The new sergeant, however, saw this as a threat. I constantly assisted him in making an ass of himself. He got to a point where he would try to divert me from hot calls because I knew how to investigate them as first responder.

One day we had a big shooting incident involving gang members. I arrived in the area as did two sergeants. There were several officers in the area so I did not inform radio that I was in the area immediately. One thing that cops do is talk on the radio too much. The idea was to get your information together and then talk on the radio as little as possible. This eliminated the air being busy if you had an emergency.

Well, when I came over the radio to make an announcement, the sergeant told me over the radio that I wasn't needed as they had enough officers in the area. I could not help myself; I had to embarrass him.

"Well," I said, "sergeant, I just wanted to inform radio that I have recovered the gun used in the incident."

He was quite miffed and backed off.

The other sergeant knew that I was a good cop, but I had worked with him as an officer. Something was different. I thought it was part of the ongoing hassle I was having with "good ole boys" (the crooked gun.)

I decided that I would try other units in the department. I had been around long enough and people knew about my work. I was considered a good cop. So I requested transfer to the motorcycle squad. I already had a motorcycle and the proper endorsements on my driver license.

My application was well received by the captain of the unit. I met him when I first came on and he knew I was an ex-Marine. I had an interview with this captain and he said that I would be in the next class of new bike riders.

When the time came for the beginning of the class, I was informed that because of my previous problems with the "fat" lieutenant, I could not be accepted into the motorcycle unit. He said that I should re-apply in six months.

I continued my patrol duties and stayed in touch with the captain of the motorcycle unit. When six months were up, I went to the captain's office. He again spoke about the "fat" lieutenant and said he could not approve my transfer. I was beginning to get a little perturbed. Something that was not a big deal was sure causing me a bit of grief. I needed a transfer and I knew I had to prepare myself. One other option was to take and pass the detective test.

In Police work, things can turn to "shit" very quickly! One of the best personal examples that I can relate is as follows: One day while reporting for patrol duty in the East precinct, my sergeant asked me if I wanted a half day off.

Well, mind you, this is Seattle in the prime of summer. Everyone who knows Seattle, knows there is no better place to be on Earth than Seattle on a sunny, summer day. It was also a Saturday afternoon and mating season at Greenlake.

So I say to the sarge, "of course, what's the catch?" He smiles and says, "Take officer ————-out and show her what police work is." I said, "oh hell no". He assured me that only one or two contacts with real criminals should suffice to give her an idea of the real dangers of real police work. I agreed.

Now this officer is question was a pretty little female who was used to guys showing up at all her calls and basically handling them for her. I just stayed away from her on the street. Wanting this day off really badly, I set out to show her some bad guys and go to the beach. We started a basic patrol of our area as we a district car. I made a normal stop at one of the local stores and chatted with the owner. He was a legend in Seattle and ran the premier tackle shop in town. I always stopped and got the latest on what fish were biting and where. After a few minutes of fish gossip, he asked me if I could move along a few of the local "druggies" that had been harassing his customers. They were about a block and half up the street. I told him I, correction, we would handle it. We got back into our patrol car and drove away in a direction away from the bad guys. I actually drove around the block and approached them from behind in an alley. There was approximately 7-8 of them and they were drinking and playing music and generally just "bullshitting". They never looked back or heard the patrol car approach. All I am actually thinking at this point is that I have a partner and we can possibly get a good arrest out of this. Psyched at this point, I look at my partner, who is scared "shitless". This is no time for a lesson. Her eyes are frozen wide open and she can't even speak. I stopped the car and exited quietly. I grabbed my five-cell flashlight, but left my 26-inch nightstick in the car. My partner did not exit when I did. I gave her a little time. I approached the group from behind and surprised them. Some fled right away. Others were deciding if they should run or not. The last couple were "high" but cool. They just stood there and we conversed about the drinking and disturbing the peace. They all agreed to leave the area, except for this one "cat" that I had never seen before. He was kind of mean. He was good size and buffed out. I quickly assessed he was fresh out of the joint (jail). He was calling me names and doing the "rooster". The other "cats" were telling him to be "cool". All the others knew me from previous encounters and knew I would battle, but I was fair. Realizing that this could turn into a problem, I made eye contact with my partner, who was still sitting in the car, looking like a deer caught in headlights. I knew not to expect any help there. I let this man run his mouth and much to my astonishment, he had two loaded syringes in his front shirt pocket. He had apparently forgotten all about them. After receiving about all that I cared to hear from this gentleman, I advised him that he was under arrest. He laughed because he thought I was kidding. I laughed because he thought I was kidding. I then very quickly, took the syringes from his pocket and showed them to him. His smile slowly went upside down. I then turned to signal my partner to come and assist; the suspect then took a swing at me. I was able to catch a glimpse of the punch as I turning back and was able to avoid the major impact of the blow; however, it caught me in the jaw. He then followed with another blow, which I was able to deflect with an upper outside block. I then naturally pivoted under the deflected blow and placed my shoulder into the small of the suspects' back. I then wrapped both my arms around the suspects' waist and lifted him over my head. As I held him in the air, I thought, "maybe this is a little much". Then I resolved with, "he hit a police officer," I then slammed him into the ground headfirst as I fell backwards. To my utter amazement, the suspect was on his feet before I was sure if he was even awake. I quickly got to my feet and the exact same scenario took place. I slammed him a little harder this time. He still got up and the fight was still on. Well, I knew that this was not your garden-variety arrest and this man was not normal. We squared off and went at it toe to toe. I hit him with very good shots and he seemed unaffected. We went down and rolled and grappled and punched and fought on and on. It didn't take long, before I was out of energy. He just kept on going. My gun came out of my holster and was spinning around on the ground. He was yelling to the others to get it and shoot me. I was yelling for them to get away from it. No one came for it. I then yelled to my horrified partner, who was still in the car, to help or call for help! She asked me for our location. It yelled out to her 1414 S. King ST., alley behind. I took my hand-held radio from my Sam Brown belt and I struck the suspect in the head with it with all my might. Blood squirted out in spurts. The suspect was not phased. He continued to fight. We were both covered in blood. It was difficult to tell whose blood was whose. I managed to get the suspect into a figure four hold from behind and place a chokehold around his neck. This was not an authorized restraint of the department at the time, but my life was in danger. Even so, the suspect would not go out (remained combative). I was in full uniform with a bulletproof vest. I had on boots and all the necessary equipment to perform my duties. I was weighed down and worn out from the fight. I was thinking that I was going to lose this fight and I was going to die that day. I was about to give up, when my young daughters' face appeared in my mind. I regained my strength and was able to hold on until back up arrived. The first officer to arrive was a former Marine and friend. He flew out of his patrol car and not knowing whose blood was whose, he made short work of the suspect. Several officers arrived and the situation was soon under control. I sat down on the ground after encounter and thanked God. I could not even consider that this female police officer considered herself qualified to be a police officer. I gathered my composure and went to my car. I was about to leave when this coward approached to get in. I did not wait. I got to the station and when she arrived, all she could do was apologize. I did not respond to her. I could only think about dying that day. It turned that this suspect was on juice (PCP). He didn't even feel most of the beating he received that day. After all the paper was done and suspect was booked, I went home. So much for a nice day at the beach. I took a few days off to recover. While I was off, I decided to join a martial arts school and get back into fighting condition. I found one right away and joined. When I returned to work the next week, I discovered that the female officer had suffered such a trauma that she was put on a desk. Shortly after she made detective in the narcotics unit. The "crooked gun" just won't go away. I was continually losing faith in the justice system and the department.

I began to study, and when I felt I was ready, I went out to the academy and took the test. It was a two-part test and it was presided over by a sergeant. This sergeant was in his own bit of controversy. He had gotten himself into some tax scam and was being prosecuted by the federal government. I had seen him around the department and had not really had any reason to know him. We were never in the same unit.

I had studied the material and I was comfortable that I was going to pass the test. I turned in part one and was ready for part two when the sergeant informed me that I had failed the first part. I was shocked and in disbelief. The test was not even hard and I breezed through it.

At first, I accepted what he had told me and I decided to take it next time. I walked out to my car and opened the door. Then it hit me like a ton of bricks. I did not fail that damn test. I turned around and marched right back into the classroom. There were still people present and testing. I walked up to the sergeant and told him my feelings. I then asked him to check my answers again. He did so reluctantly.

I looked over his shoulder and watched as he realized that he had marked thirteen answers wrong in a row. He placed the answer key over the answer side and discovered that all thirteen of those answers were correct.

He then said nothing, but "Oh."

He gave me part two. I sat down and completed part two in much the same manner as part one. When I took it to the sergeant for grading, he appeared to grade it and simply said that I failed and he would not allow me to see the scoring.

Time went on and about a year later I applied for a transfer to the harbor unit. I liked the water, was a good swimmer, and really wanted to learn all about boating and marine issues. You see, after all, I am and have always been an avid fisherman, even bought my own little boat.

As I was watching the movement all around the department, I just couldn't get a break. I was a good cop and couldn't buy a transfer (figure of speech). After being told that I couldn't have a transfer to harbor patrol because of the "fat lieutenant," some action was required.

I wasn't going to take it anymore. I started to gather information on how to get action through outside mediation; in other words, I wanted to know if I could sue the department.

I was referred to the City of Seattle Human Rights Department, one look around that office and, thanks, but no thanks. I checked out the county office, same. I didn't trust anyone to have my best interests at heart.

I remembered this guy that my brother had told me about from Detroit. He was a big time lawyer who had done work for the ACLU. He was now living in the Seattle area. I contacted him and we met.

He was an impressive brother, but after a couple of meetings, I decided not to go with him. My experience on the police department proved to me that lawyers talk a lot about what they can do, but don't do very much. Besides I would have to trust this person with some very personal feelings about issues that I was afraid to discuss with anyone. You see, black people understand that if you talk about racism and mistreatment enough, your personal situation is defused. So, the best way to get it out there was, surprise, no talking about what I was going to do and to just do it!

So now totally stumped, I looked in the phone book and came across the Washington State Human Rights Commission. It was right down the street from the police department. I had already arrived at work early that day so I parked my car and went to my sergeant and asked for the day off.

No one really knew that I was pissed about these things yet so he gave me the day off. I took my little files with me down the street. I walked into the office and there I met this white woman.

She identified herself as an investigator. I reluctantly sat down with her and slowly began to give her little bits of information. I was watching her reaction. I think she recognized my untrusting eye. She did not try to convince me that she was "good." She did say after about two hours of listening to me that she thought I had a good complaint. She assured me that if we wrote it up, it was not going to disappear or be mishandled. I felt that I could trust her.

We spent the whole morning and part of her lunch hour typing it up. When we finished, I was nervous and asked as I was about to leave, "What about retaliation from the department when they find out about the complaint?"

She said they would not find out until they received the formal complaint and it would have a clause in it about no retaliation.

It took about a week for the department to be notified. Oh boy, I was immediately placed in "no mans" land. The black officers treated me like I was the troublemaker, making it harder on all blacks. The white officers treated me like I was some radical black with no reason to complain about anything. Although it was nothing overt, I got many messages and was pretty much on my own.

It was at this time that I took up another martial art and went back to college. I pretty much got away from police officers as social partners.

The investigator stayed in touch with me regularly.

She knew the different stages that I would go through and supported me. She said that they had heard many stories about the way the police conducted business, but no one would follow through with complaints.

Well, it took over a year, but my complaint was upheld and I was given the right to sue the police department by the State of Washington. I was tired of the whole thing and simple asked for my choice of the assignments that I was wrongfully denied and a letter of apology. I received and accepted these things and went on with my career.

Now that I had successfully confronted the practices of the department, the black officers came around again and acted like they were my best friends. They acted like "we beat them." I never trusted another one of them during my time on the department. Although I never said a word to them about it, they could read how I felt about them.

I did assist some of the younger officers with some of their problems. I was not trying to be a sea lawyer, because that was a no-win situation. The department knew that I would fight, so they left me alone for awhile.

I chose to go into the harbor patrol. I went out there and was not received with open arms, as you might expect, but I was on the "treat with kit gloves list." The officer who was in charge of training me didn't want to be anywhere near me. You see, this was a good ole boy job too. They had a couple of tokens hidden out there, but the mainstream were good ole boys. Well, I was learning despite the royal treatment. It was said that I was having difficulty learning to drive the boats, but the little woman who went out with me was doing just fine, not.

They tried to make it uncomfortable out there for me, but I paid my dues to be there and I was not going anywhere. After they realized that I was not going anywhere, all of a sudden they realized that I was on the detective's list (the crooked gun). They offered me a job in a unit where they put most of the blacks who make detective and they didn't want them to be seen or get the opportunity to shine. They tell you that is where you get experience investigating. Mind you, the white detective must be born to investigate, because they rarely have stop in burglary on their way to the top.

Well, I took the job because I was going to accept any challenge they threw at me and do well. I went to work for a captain who was good to work for. The lieutenant was even better. He and I got along great. He was an outdoorsman and I liked the outdoors too. He liked that I was an ex-Marine and I felt that he respected me and knew that I could do the job. After a while he gave me special assignments and I accomplished the goals of those assignments.

After that, I was assigned to another undercover assignment, this time as a real detective. I worked with different federal agencies and had a pretty normal working experience, if you call the life of an undercover cop normal.

I enjoyed living on the edge and matching wits with criminals.

After awhile, it was time for a change. I put in for a transfer to the juvenile section. I worked with another brother. We had worked together in burglary before I left to go undercover. He had no desire to go there. We worked well together and put a lot of time in the community. We had some of the same ideas about not locking up the young blacks all the time, but going to their homes and having group family talks and figuring out ways to stop the criminal behavior. It worked sometimes.

During this time, I was also selected to be an instructor at the police academy. I gave classes to new officers in juvenile procedures. I had received training in instructor development and many other areas, but when full-time positions came available at the academy, the positions were still given to less experienced white officers.

In the years that I was in the U.S. Marine Corps, I had been a general's driver. I had experience handling dignitaries and VIPs. I planned itineraries and handled personal and business functions.

When the driver for the mayor of Seattle was retiring, there was a department-wide search for a qualified candidate to replace him. I had not heard anything about this opportunity until my captain approached me one day and asked me if I was applying for the mayor's driver position.

I said, "No."

He said that I should because he could not think of anyone more qualified than I. I told him that I would.

He said he would submit my application. I completed my application and went to the captain's office to submit the package to him, but he was not available. The same black sergeant who had helped the "good ole boys" against me in 1985 was temporarily in charge. There was a deadline and it was close and the sergeant said he would submit my application. I gave it to him and forgot about it.

I saw the captain about two weeks later and he asked me if I had applied. I told him that I had looked for him, but after I couldn't find him, I gave it to the sergeant.

He said, "Oh no."

He explained to me that the "black officer association" of which I was not a member, had their own agenda. He doubted that my application had been submitted. This white captain knew more about the black politics on the department than I did. I told my partner, who had gotten the part-time job as the mayor's driver, that I knew what had happened. It was a political position because you had the mayor's ear. I was not much into politics, and this was not an issue worth pursuing.

My martial arts training was going pretty good at this time, and my commitment unwavering. With the blessing of my TaeKwonDo master, I opened my own TaeKwonDo School in the central area of Seattle. It was a predominantly black neighborhood, although many Mexicans, whites and Asians lived there. There were gangs right outside the door, but we moved them a few doors down. They didn't mess with our students or interfere with our school. Basically, we learned how to co-exist. I enjoyed teaching children. Although adults, civilian and cops, were coming, I focused on the children. I had quietly decided to re-prioritize. Police work was not satisfying anymore. I could help my community by helping to produce children with confidence and self-respect.

I would tell kids that we came in contact with about the school and I had special programs for kids with financial or physical and emotional problems. I had an all-around school. I had police officers coming to the school for classes. I had former gang members as students.

I had teachers from local public schools coming to me and telling me how their students were becoming better students as a result of the rules at my school. This was very satisfying to me as a teacher.

I found that I was handling family problems between students and parents. I discovered that as a martial arts teacher, I was a counselor.

One of my young students was twelve years old. He was from a troubled family with an extensive police history. His grandmother brought him into my school as the children's class was in progress. He came in with his little gang banger attitude. I immediately threw him out. The grandmother was a little shocked.

I explained to her that we were going to work on his attitude. I explained a little to her about how the martial arts worked. It was all about respect for self and others. She understood and agreed to send him back the next day.

He walked in as class began. He was late. I told him to leave.

He said, "What?"

I told him to get there on time and buy his uniform so he could be ready when class started. He bought the uniform at that time. He walked in the next class in his uniform, but was about one minute late. I sent him away again. He was furious. After about one and a half weeks from the time he first walked into my school, he had his first class. He beamed and took to all aspects of training. I received letters from his teachers and his grandmother.

After seven months, I allowed several of my students to attend their first championship. It was the state championship. I knew that my previous teachers would be there. I prepared my students and we went. After the first couple of matches, the announcers were declaring winners from "Simba's TaeKwonDo." I can't tell you how proud I was when that same young man was declared the Washington state champion.

I wasn't much for holding onto girlfriends. My focus was my work and my TaeKwonDo. Seattle is the kind of town that you have to know people or where and when to go places. I had my favorite spot. It was called the "Scarlet Tree." It was a jazz restaurant with live jazz-fusion, some of the greats. I loved the "Tree." They liked me too or at least gave me that illusion. I was a regular for more than seventeen years. The Tree was my spot.

I had broken up a few fights there and helped a little here and there. There was a drug problem in the Tree when I first started going there. I liked the place so I wasn't leaving. They got used to me and the dopers faded away.

One Saturday I spent my day cleaning my home. I was just being domestic. I made dinner and had wine all by myself. I like to do that sometimes. Really, I don't want to be around women sometimes. So this particular night, after my meal and I all was settled down for the evening, I decided to go to the Tree for a little jazz. I got dressed and was looking good. I drove down to the Tree. It was only about five minutes from my house.

I got there and looked around and ordered my drink. I walked around and spotted two attractive females sitting alone. I approached and bought them drinks. I asked and they allowed me to sit down. We started talking and we danced a little. I selected one of the two and we started to hit it off. I asked them to join me for breakfast and they agreed. Then I told them that I was a policeman and asked what they did. I gave them my business card at that point.

The one that I was interested in told me that her husband was a firefighter. First of all, I was surprised At how nonchalant she was about being married. I was not interested in a firefighter's wife or anyone else's wife for that matter. I retrieved my card and said thanks, but no thanks. I did however agree to walk them to their car.

All was well and I was saying goodbye when a car pulled up and blocked their cars in. A large black male drove the car with a chubby white female in the passenger seat. They just sat there and smirked at me. I asked them to please move. They did not respond. I walked away toward the phone booth and told them that I would call the police. The female said something derogatory about my manhood.

I said, "Whatever, Chubby."

She came unglued. She came out of the car and attacked me. I backed away as she swung at me over and over. Finally her escort exited the car and I told him to get control of his woman. He laughed and told me that I had to handle her. She kept attacking. The male then approached me from the side. I knew he was going to try to blindside me.

When he got closer, I took my eyes off of her for a moment and one of her punches hit me in my mouth. I deflected her next punches and gave her a twist of the wrist. She went down and rolled on the ground. I then faced the man and he put up his hands to fight. I could tell from his body and hand position that he did not have experience. He was just intimidating because of his size.

I told him that I was a black belt and I could tell he did not know how to fight. He walked toward me and I threw a roundhouse kick to the right side of his head with a short finishing technique to the body. I don't intend to tell a war story, but this is what happened. I took the fight out of the man. I called the police to make an incident report because there had actually been a physical confrontation.

It turned out that the woman had received a bruised wrist and the man a fractured rib and dislocated shoulder.

The police came and I had to go to the station and make a statement. There were witnesses to this incident and I was still treated like a criminal by the department. I knew that I did nothing wrong, but months went by and I never received notice from Internal Investigations. I had another incident about three months later, in which a man in a local grocery store attacked me. The clerks knew me and saw the whole thing.

I subdued this man without much effort and suddenly remembered that I was being investigated for an assault.

I let the man go because I did not want to have another incident suggesting I was heavy-handed.

I went to Internal Investigations to find out what had happened to the previous case. I was stonewalled. I went to the prosecutor's office and the assistant prosecutor told me that the sergeant from Internal Investigations had submitted the case to them three times for charges against me.

I was furious and I went to the chief of police. I explained to him my recent incident and the fact that I felt unsafe having to worry about handling the streets and the possibility of physical confrontation at every turn. I began to feel paranoid.

He was in total agreement with at me and called Internal Investigations. He expressed his dissatisfaction with this kind of treatment and said resolve immediately.

I really began to get disillusioned with the system. I started to feel targeted again by some of the good ole boys and leaned more and more toward leaving the department.

I got more involved with martial arts in the state of Washington. I associated mainly with Korean masters and practitioners of the arts. When my friend was killed after a night of big narcotics raids, I was really disturbed. He had finished for the night and was going home. Three young men tried to carjack him and killed him. He was able to return fire and wounded one of them.

The department called him a detective in death, but would only call him "officer" in life. This disgusted me because I remembered that when I was an undercover officer I worked so hard for that detective shield. They made it so hard for me to get it. Then they turned around and called him "detective" in the media. "WOW".

I worked a couple of good cases before I left. One was a case where someone stole a defibrillator off of an aid car. I was not interested in prosecuting the suspect; I wanted the suspect(s) to understand that this piece of equipment was vital to the black community. The city was not going to rush and replace it, and what if the grandmother of the suspect had a heart attack one night?

I went to the media and they were good enough to air my thoughts. I received a call that same day and recovered the defibrillator.

My supervisor then wanted me to pursue the suspect after I said publicly that I would not. I refused. This was my way of trying to get better relations between the police department and the community. It was working; I was making a difference.

I got tired of watching police reports come through and little black kids were getting police records for doing little kid things and white kids were being sent home for the same activities with no record. I was getting tired of this double standard and no one else seemed to care.

I started to invite kids to come to my school of martial arts and I gave some free lessons. I gave them something to do that would make them feel good about themselves. It was a popular school. I used my position as instructor at the academy to emphasize to new officers the need to be fair with juveniles

When some of the rookies that I was instructing heard my name in class, they told me that stories were being told to them about some of my successful cases in narcotics. This was a surprise to me. Why didn't someone tell me that I did a good job?

The last good case that I had before I left was an Asian organized crime case. I was and had been a member of an international investigators group. We investigated Asian organized crime activity between the U.S. and Canada. I had certain information and profiles for these people. One day I located a suspicious male. He was the picture profile. I watched him for a while and finally made contact.

He allowed me into his apartment and I saw tens of thousands of dollars worth of electronic equipment, musical equipment, telephone equipment and weapons. I made three arrests and recovered the equipment. It was stolen from Canada, Oregon and California. This case was big. My sergeant was very proud as he turned it over to the FBI.

Now this sergeant was a piece of work. He was a thirty-five-year veteran. He had a reputation for being one of the biggest rednecks on the department. I had been in the juvenile squad in the central area of town that included downtown as well. The north squad had an opening and I lived in the north part of town. My partner told me not to go out there to work for him, because he was known to hate blacks. I knew I was good at my job and if it came down to more than that I would deal with that then.

I called him up on the phone and told him that I wanted an interview with him. He told me to come on down. I went to talk to him. He pulled no punches. He told me he knew I was a good cop and he would be glad to have me. He expected me to carry my load. I transferred and we became friends. We fished together and ate meals together. I went to his home, met his family. I never judge a person by what others tell me. I give people a chance. It is the best way.

I never heard another word about the case, but I was proud. My mother who still lived in Charlotte, North Carolina was also proud of me and she made me my favorite cake. It was a pineapple cake. This was my special cake when I was growing up. It was not like a pineapple upside down cake. She sent the cake UPS and it arrived the next day at the office.

I opened the box and placed it on the table in the coffee room. Then I went to the bathroom to rinse off a knife to cut the cake. I was gone for less than five minutes and when I returned, the entire cake was gone. Not even a crumb. No one would admit to eating any of it. That is how cops are about "sweets." I called my mom and we laughed about it.

My mother died a few months later.

Early one Saturday morning my phone rang. It was my brother. I could tell by his voice that something was wrong. He told me that my mother was in a coma and I should come home. I jumped up and immediately packed some things and asked my girlfriend to get me a flight. I didn't speak much. I focused only on getting myself home.

I arrived and my mother was still in a coma. I held her hand and talked to her. She would acknowledge me by squeezing my fingers. I had to go home to shower, and when I got to the house, the phone rang. She had passed away. I flew back to the hospital.

This devastated me. I completely fell apart. It was not real. I could do nothing to stop the pain.

My siblings were trying to plan the estate and settle things the next day. I became incensed and told them that I was not interested in any of it because my mother was not even in the ground. I have been angry with them since. It was childish but I had to be angry with someone. I returned to Seattle and my job, but I wasn't comfortable anymore.

I think that "crooked gun" in the beginning was a sign that my police career would be unpredictable. I would learn who I really was and that there would be some curves along the way. To protect and serve applies to everyone. There is no black and white in law enforcement; there is just "law." If you decide to be a cop, then be a cop. Stand up for right.

Afterward

When the idea of this book entered my mind, I didn't quite know how to proceed. Several titles crossed my mind. When I first joined the department, or you might say, when I was hired, I was issued a gun with a crooked barrel. I thought about several cop authors who told about their experiences in ways that were just unrealistic to me. I thought about my own fourteen plus years experience as a police officer. I had some real wild experiences, but most of my experiences were everyday life where some people just needed assistance.

I had received between twenty to thirty letters of commendations from the citizens that I had served, and not many from the department. That was okay because I was not, nor have I ever been, a brown-nose type. I was proud to be that professional police officer.

I wanted to tell my story not as some hero cop, which I am not, but I think there are some citizens in the city of Seattle that can remember something good about their experience with this police officer.

You see, every cop who does it right is a hero. Not Mel Gibson, Will Smith, Martin Lawrence, Stallone or Snipes or even my favorite, Steven Seagal — these guys are good at their trade, but they are actors. We don't go around shooting up people and blowing up cities and passing the paper on to some less important people. We start and work our cases until the last "i" is dotted and the last "t" is crossed. A real case is won in court.

A professional police officer knows how to do his job. That includes identifying, collecting, protecting, and submitting evidence, conducting proper interviews, and regarding all known information before pulling that trigger on the street.

Many young police officers can't wait to prove that they can pull that trigger. The truth is that most regret it afterward — good shooting or not. You see, the shooting is only the beginning. There are many victims in a shooting. The actual victim, the person who shoots him, the families of both, the witnesses, the communities, the department — the list goes on. So no real cop is interested in having a body count.

I received several of my letters of commendations for not pulling the trigger and using restraint. I attribute the ability to use restraint and judgment to many years of martial arts training. Violence, fighting or any degree of force is based on situation control, not just domination. A justified shooting, for example, simply means you won't have legal problems if you shoot, but the personal issues can be much more devastating to everyone involved.

Real cops are not recognized as heroes until something happens to them as in the case of my friend. We go out and do the job every day. We go where others fear to go. We see what others dare not see. We speak of the unmentionable. We resolve the irresolvable. We deprive people of their freedom and free others. We receive far more criticism than praise. Being a police officer is not a job, it is a way of life.

"To protect and serve" may be a cliché, but it is the personal commitment of every police officer, man or woman, who takes pride in this profession and does it right.

I never had any bad experiences with police officers while I was growing up, besides my mother would have broken my neck. In my house growing up, you always respected parents first, then God, then other adults. Outside the house, preachers, teachers, police, neighborhood adults — "the village" — raised us.

I am a product of America. My grandfather was a Cherokee Indian. My great-grandmother was white; even then there were interracial relationships. My grandfather was a large man of good looks and strong features. He was a hard man, but fair to his children and wife. He had been much older than his wife, but together they had twelve children. My mother was the eleventh child. Ironically, so am I.

My father, I don't know much about. This is not the typical story of a black man not handling his responsibility. My father and mother had eleven children together and my father provided for his family until I was four years old. He served in the United States Navy in the war and raised all of his kids up until he and my mother divorced.

I have but a few memories of my father, but I hold him in high regard. My father and his older brother had been raised by an aunt and uncle. For the place and times, they were of substance. He had been a farmer, and adhering to the wishes of my mother, he moved the family to the city. My father was a proud man and had trouble adjusting to working for others, especially in the South. I am still researching my father.

So my book, my story, my life if you will, is not about racism, discrimination, didn't have, couldn't have. It is about character development, self-pride, honor and most importantly, riding out the "storm of life" while maintaining these traits.

It is an American's story, an American made up of all that America is. I am African American. I am Native American. I am Caucasian American. I am the Declaration of Independence. I am The United States Constitution. I am America. To further discriminate against anyone is to discriminate against all of us. I am tired, but I will fight until the end. Keep me poor, talk negatively about me, call me names, but my dignity and character are intact.

I can't say enough about the martial arts. I began practice in my teens with no idea that I would make it my life and philosophy. The studies have helped me endure the trials of life and remain strong. When I have had weak moments along the way, I have had my own trinity to get me through. Through God, I know that I am a part of him and his family of life. Through my mother, from my mother, I learned unconditional love and self worth. From the martial arts, instructors, and practitioners that I have known over the last twenty-nine years, I have learned that the only limits in this life are the ones you place on yourself. The tenets of martial arts are the tenets of life.

About the Author

Waleed SimBa was born with a very strong spirit. He believes the combination of Native American and African American heritage is instrumental in his lifelong pursuit of self-awareness. As a teen he began his martial arts journey and hasn't looked back. He knew there was something to the in the spiritual suggestions that came early in training. He continues to train with masters in Korea, Singapore and the United States is always ready to learn more about himself.

Mr. SimBa feels that martial arts and the United States Marine Corps provided the foundation that was necessary for the discipline and execution for his duties as an undercover police officer/detective. That same combination has provided the character and honor necessary to overcome the challenges of today.

Printed in the United States
19215LVS00001B/73-90